The sound of heavy, snorted breaths rung down the hall, and the slow sound of hoof beats grew closer. A huge black beast nosed its' way through the door, its' hooves striking sparks off the polished floor. The Chimera rode leisurely into the throne room, his eyes fixed on the defiant king.

"And who will you hide behind, now?" he demanded. The king raised his chin.

"I hide from neither man nor beast. Nor Hell spawn!" he spat. The Chimera raised an eyebrow. The sword in the king's hand began to shift. The blade suddenly shot backward, piercing his throat with vipers' teeth. In horror, the king let go of the snakes tail and clutched at its' fanged mouth. The tail whipped around his neck and chest and began to squeeze. The king struggled, his face a mottled purple, his tongue rolling out of blue lips. His eyes bulged and he made a desperate, gasping sound, and then fell forward onto the floor. The Chimera watched as the snake uncoiled and began to swallow the body.

"And so shall I swallow the world," he assured the horse, patting its' neck.

This book is a work of fiction. Any resemblance to any person, alive or dead, is coincidental.

For Brandea, you mean more than you know and helped more than you can ever dream. Thanks for rekindling a broken dream.

ISBN 978-0-6151-6664-3

The Chimera

By Kathryn H Sargeant

Chapter One

Dust fell from the ceiling, powdering on the smooth floor. The walls groaned like beasts overburdened. Somewhere ahead the darkness pulsed, a black heartbeat of death. The ceiling above shrieked in protest as a dim light formed around a square in the rocks. Tiles that had been cemented together for hundreds of years shook loose in a mighty downward rush. They lay broken and piled upon one another in a heap. Coughing from above the hole, then a single torch dropped into the chasm. A head poked through the hole and looked around.

"Loud enough to wake the dead, don't you think?" he grinned back up at his companions. Someone grunted.

"For our sakes, I hope not," a male voice answered lightly. The head disappeared to be replaced by a rope and a pair of legs. Slowly, the three lowered themselves down into the passage below, until they stood in a semi-circle around the burning torch. The two men were tall and lean but that is where the similarities ended. Where one was fair, with long blonde hair pulled back in a tight braid, the other was dark with hair cut short. The light from the flickering torch cast deep shadows across their faces, lending them a corpselike air. The woman standing between them shuddered and then grinned nervously.

"Tell me why we are here, again, Malcolm," she said, brushing back her unruly long auburn hair. She adjusted her headband, tucking the offending lock behind its leather lacings. The darker man smiled.

"A hundred bloodstones and a hundred moonstones for an old hunk of silver," he reminded her. "Enough money to start an inn somewhere they have never even heard of snow."

"Oh, yeah. Now, I remember," she grinned reaching for the torch. She lifted it high overhead and looked at the strange carvings on the walls. She frowned at them, uncertainly. "Does this say here be ducks?"

"Here lies the Chimera. Long may he burn in Hell. Weep, children of the lost, for you shall suffer a worse fate if you dare to disturb his rest," the fair one read over her head. "Sounds like a real cheery sort, if you ask me."

"Grams would be so proud of how you are using your education, Jackie," Malcolm sniffed. "Don't you think so, Kari?"

"Which way?" she growled. Jackie pointed down the dark passageway to her right. She turned and started into the darkness.

"Wait!" Jackie called, and she stopped. He pulled two torches from his belt loops and held them out. "I'm afraid of the dark."

Wordlessly, she held out her burning torch and lit his. He handed a torch to Malcolm and then turned to inspect the walls. There were carvings of gargoyles, trolls, hounds, all with cheeks puffed as if they were blowing air through mangled lips. Kari turned and started down the tunnel again.

"Kari, drop!"

She flattened herself to the cold dusty floor just as a score of darts flew from the carved jaws on the wall. Malcolm whistled softly. Jackie grinned, pulling his pack from his back. He dug through the contents and came out with a small quail.

"How did you keep that thing quiet and in there?" Malcolm demanded.

"I asked it nicely. Stay down, Kari, I'm going to try to set off the other darts," Jackie called. He tossed a handful of corn onto the passage floor in front of her head and let the quail go. It ran in hopping steps all over the floor, gobbling up every piece of corn it came to. Darts twanged over her head and Kari lay deathly still. The quail hopped up on her back, trilling happily, then jumped over her head.

"Is that all of them?" she asked.

"I think so. You can get up, now," Jackie called, digging more corn out of his pocket. He shouldered his pack and they walked to where she was standing, the quail darting in and out from between her legs. Jackie tossed the corn further down the corridor and the quail took off, happily. "See? No more darts."

A clang of oiled metal resounded through the passage as razor toothed saws shot up from the floor and out from the walls at ankle and knee level. The quail squeaked as a blade tore through its tiny body, spraying blood and feathers against the wall. Kari raised an eyebrow at him.

"Uhm, anyone know how to levitate?" Jackie asked, sheepishly. Kari looked over the walls. Carved into them about an inch over the highest blade openings and then five feet above those were niches. Kari crushed her torch out in the dust of the floor and secured the stick to her belt.

"How about we do the next best thing?" she asked, setting her foot in the first niche and leaping to catch the handhold. Her foot grazed the opening and the blade flashed out, narrowly missing her heel. She began slowly to climb sideways down the tunnel. "Hold your torches out as far as you dare. I don't want any surprises at the other end." Jackie looked at Malcolm and shrugged, then threw his torch end over end as far down the passage as he could. It whizzed past Kari's head and she almost lost her grip on the handhold above her head. She glared at him over her shoulder. "Stop screwing around!"

"Sorry," he muttered. They watched as she traveled slowly down the tunnel for a good length and then suddenly stopped. "What's wrong?"

"Ran out of holes," she called back.

"What are you waiting for?" Malcolm asked and Jackie slapped his shoulder.

"You to come give me a big wet kiss," she snarled, leaping from the wall with a mighty sideways push. She landed in a tense crouch, head and shoulders hunched against the expected slash of blades. None came. Jackie inspected the toeholds and looked at his feet. "Wait, let me see what's down here," Kari pulled the torch and flint box from her belt and relit the torch, holding it high overhead. She scrutinized the walls for a long time before nodding. "I think I found something."

She slid her hand into the mouth of a large carved lion, closing her fingers around one of its large teeth, and pushed. Blades whirred from overhead, slicing down the center and sides of the passage. "Ooops." She grinned apologetically and pulled the tooth back toward her. There was a grinding sound from inside the walls and then silence. Malcolm looked at Jackie.

"After you," he said. Jackie shook his head, digging into his pack once more. He brought out a ripe melon, perfectly round, and rolled it down the corridor. Nothing happened. He sauntered after the melon, snatching it and the torch up as he passed them. Malcolm followed a few steps behind. "How did you know that would work, Kari?"

"Seemed wrong. Cats don't have snaggly fangs in the back of their mouths," she shrugged. "Anybody have a clue what's next?" Silence. Kari shrugged and started slowly off down the passage. The carvings on the wall gave way to intermittent dragon heads, mouths outstretched in angry roars, and the floor changed from smooth stone to lettered tiles. Kari turned to Malcolm.

"Any ideas what this is supposed to be?" she demanded. He shook his head.

"Maybe we're supposed to spell something?" Jackie offered. Malcolm snapped his fingers.

"Chimera! I'll bet we're supposed to spell Chimera!" he started to step out onto the C tile that was two spaces ahead of him but Kari caught his shoulder.

"Wait! Jackie, let me see that melon," she snapped. He handed it over reluctantly, and she tossed it onto the C tile. A blast of flames erupted from a dragonhead, scorching the tile and roasting the melon on the spot. Malcolm shuddered. "We have to think about this. What is a chimera?"

"A legend?" Malcolm offered. "A nightmare?"

"It's a lion head and a dragon body," Jackie added, thoughtfully.

"Jackie, do you have anything else in that pack?" Kari asked, chewing her lower lip. He dug through and came up with a large ball of twine. She took it and looked at the first line of tiles before her feet. "We came through the lion; now let's see if we can enter the dragon. Which one does dragon start with?" Jackie pointed and she dropped the twine on the tile marked with D and jumped back. Nothing happened. She looked at Jackie, who shrugged.

"I know! I'll go first this time!" he offered with forced enthusiasm. He stepped onto the D tile and snatched up the twine, placing it carefully back into his pack. He searched the tiles before him and then stepped onto the R. "Two over, one up." Slowly, they followed him, calling back tile placements to the one behind over their shoulders. When they finally made it across, Jackie sniffed righteously. "You really should learn to read."

"Bite me," Kari snapped. She began examining the dragon sculptures along the wall. "Ah-hah! Dragons shouldn't have human tongues." She reached in and pressed the tongue down and the tunnel behind them filled with flames that quickly burned themselves out. She straightened her shoulders and set off again. The corridor turned sharply to the left, ending suddenly in a huge gold door with a chimera engraved in its surface. The lion head was devouring a maiden while the dragon tail was crushing a church. The land was cast in ruin about the figure. Kari shivered. "Well, here we are."

"Yep, here we are," Malcolm agreed. "Now, how do we get in there?"

Jackie studied the door, thoughtfully.

"Are those gems in that maiden's chest?" he asked. Kari nodded. "And there are gems in the outspread wing right there, and in the church steeple, here. What if we were to push all three at the same time?"

"Worth a shot. Only thing it can do is kill us, right?" Malcolm shrugged. They each moved to place their fingers on the gems; Kari at the maiden, Malcolm at the wing, and Jackie at the church. "One, two, three." They pushed. With a groan, the door shook and then swung outward.

"Lay me!" Kari breathed as the light from the torches reflected off the silver coated interior of the chamber. She stepped inside her eyes growing wide. Silver piled in the corners, adorned the walls, and hung from spikes in the ceiling. Ahead of them, stretched out on a bier, lay a perfectly preserved body. Malcolm began shoving handfuls of silver into his pouches while Jackie searched the walls for clues, but Kari found herself drawn to the body. The young man was raven haired, with a beard that cut across his cheeks in a perfect line, traced his jaw and covered his chin. The rest of his face was smooth and tan, unlined by time. She ran her finger across his muscled chest and down one bulging arm. He looked more asleep than dead to her, his hands clutching the dragon carved hilt of a curved sword that rested against his stomach. Dressed in black leather, he took her breath away. "I'll bet you were something."

"Who you talking to?" Jackie asked, finally coming over to investigate the body. He looked down at the man and shuddered violently. "If that's the Chimera, shouldn't he be all withered and stuff?"

"I guess. Maybe all that silver kept him fresh. Like a jar seal," Kari shrugged. "Hey, Malcolm, how are we supposed to know which piece of silver to take?"

"The man who hired me said it would be inside the tunic of the body, right above the heart," he said, walking up beside her. She frowned.

"I don't know, Malcolm. There's a difference between robbing a tomb and robbing a body. That just isn't right."

"What's he going to use it for? Besides, think Kari. No more frozen toes. No more thankless jobs for other slobs. Finally, a place we can call home and not have to put up with anyone's crap. Somewhere warm and safe and ours," Malcolm cajoled. Kari smiled.

"You're right. We need it more than he does," she reached down the neck of the body's tunic, her fingers sliding over the smooth flesh. "This is so on beyond creepy."

"Do you feel it?" Jackie demanded excitedly. She dug deeper.

"Wait a minute…yes! I have it, but it's stuck. Help me, Jackie," Jackie wrapped his arms around her waist and gave a mighty tug. The silver held for a moment, then slid free and she pulled it from the tunic. Blood dripped from the sharpened end of the nail she held. "Eeeew!"

"Great job! Let's go." Malcolm snatched it from her hand and shoved it into Jackie's pack. Kari nodded in agreement and started toward the door. The body behind them gave a sudden great sigh. "What was that?"

They turned. The hands on the sword hilt tightened, and the corpse's eyes fluttered open. His head turned toward them and steely black eyes fixed on Kari. It smiled, pearly teeth flashing in the dusky skin.

"My thanks, little lovely. That feels much better," he said. Kari screamed. Jackie and Malcolm shoved her through the door, slamming it closed as the man sat up and swung his leg off the table.

"Run!" Jackie commanded needlessly as they pounded back down the corridor. They turned the corner, hearing the door behind them open. Malcolm tripped, sprawling in front of Kari, and they all landed in a tangle of bodies. Silver rolled across the floor and a burst of flames scorched the tiles. "I thought we turned that off!"

"It must be a timed trigger!" Kari shoved Jackie off her and dove for the dragon's head. She shoved down the tongue and the hall filled with flames. The instant they died, the trio ran for it. Kari grabbed the lion's tooth on the run and yanked. They raced down the hall and somersaulted across the dart-triggered floor.

"Little lovely, your liege is not yet in shape for this type of game. I command you to stop!"

Kari looked over her shoulder. He stood illumined by some strange green light at the first dragon's head. Kari leapt for the rope and quickly pulled herself up and out of the hole. The boys followed quickly, hearing a rush of flame from the corridor behind them. They pulled the rope up and grabbed hold of the guide wire they had strung, running back through the labyrinth they had solved earlier to the great set of carved stone doors that framed an early morning sunrise. Kari lit the twine with her torch, tossing it in as an afterthought. They threw themselves onto their waiting mounts and galloped away.

"What in the nine hells just happened?" Malcolm demanded, hunching close to his horses neck.

"Did we just do what I think we did?" Jackie shouted. "Oh, my god! Oh, my god! Did we just *wake* the Chimera?"

"No! It was a trick! Some last mental mind fuck by whoever guarded that thing! Probably some drugged dust. Yes, drug dust we kicked up with our footsteps. We all had the same vision because of the creepiness of the situation," Kari reasoned, laughing hysterically. They raced through the overgrown forest leaping over fallen trees and underbrush.

"Slow down!" Malcolm cried suddenly and they reigned in hard. Panting, he looked from one to the other. "These horses are on loan, if we lame them, we lose what little we made on this. Besides, we're running from nothing." Kari nodded and started her horse off at a more sedate pace. They rode beside her, three friends out for a casual ride.

In the tomb behind them, the Chimera stepped into the sunlight for the first time in seven hundred years. He breathed deeply of the moist spring air, gazing off in the direction they had ridden. He absently massaged the hole in his chest that even now was healing itself closed.

He smiled.

Chapter Two

Malcolm looked around the common room, squinting in the dim interior. There, in the back, someone waved to him. He moved through the crowd to the secluded table and slid into the bench across from a cowled figure. The hood inclined courteously toward him in greeting.

"Did you acquire it?" a thin, raspy voice hissed. Malcolm nodded.

"Show me the payment," he insisted. A skeletal hand reached across the table, the skin no more than tissue stretched taught across sticks. Malcolm could have crushed it easily had he wanted, but Malcolm wanted what the hand held. A medium sized pouch plunked down on the table in front of him. He crooked the mouth open with his finger and the stones inside rattled and gleamed in the torchlight. Malcolm nodded, satisfied, and slid a leather wrapped bundle across the table. The skeletal hand plucked the binding cord off and flipped back the edge. The silver nail flashed brilliantly before he covered it again.

"Good. Good," the figure chuckled, sliding the parcel into its cowl. It rose to leave, and then paused. "Tell me, did you see anything interesting when you pulled the nail free?"

Malcolm shuddered.

"It moved," Malcolm whispered. The figure tensed with excitement.

"Only moved, nothing else?" it demanded.

"It spoke to us."

"And what did it say?"

"Something like 'Thank you, little lovely. That feels good.' or maybe it was 'better'."

"Anything more?"

"It told Kari to stop, it wasn't in any shape to chase her," Malcolm stuffed the pouch inside his tunic and rose. "She's convinced it was drugged dust we kicked up off the floor or some illusion cooked up by the people who buried it."

"She's very smart, your Kari. It was, indeed, an illusion," the figure assured him.

"Well, it was a pleasure doing business with you. Your animals are outside."

"Keep the beasts. For not warning you about the illusion." It moved swiftly toward the back of the inn and disappeared through the kitchen doors. Malcolm slipped back through the crowd to the front doors and burst outside into the clean cool air. Kari looked up from dusting off her breeches.

"Well?" she asked, hesitantly.

"He said it was an illusion, that's all. And we can keep the horses," he gestured excitedly. Jackie whooped happily, scratching his mounts brown ears.

"The payment, Malcolm. Did you get the payment?" she insisted, her blue eyes shiny and intense.

"Right here," he assured her, patting his tunic.

"Then, let's get out of here," she snapped, swinging herself into the saddle. "We can pick up supplies somewhere else." Jackie and Malcolm exchanged puzzled looks, but mounted up. She turned her mount southward and they followed.

"Aren't we going to get our things from the inn?" Jackie asked, perplexed.

"I didn't leave anything I can't live without. Did you?"

"Well, no," he admitted slowly.

"Good." She spurred her horse toward the edge of town.

The footmen grumbled in annoyance, hacking and slashing at the dense foliage. The going was slow and their master was growing impatient in the stuffy confines of the old forest. His horse pawed the ground restlessly behind them. Skeletal hands clutched the reins. The waiting was physical anguish to the figure on the horse. He had been waiting a lifetime, already, and now the culmination of a family dream was close at hand. His children would be kings, fingers of a god on earth and he: he would be the guidance behind the god. One of the footmen gasped.

"I hear someone coming, my lord," he called. The man atop the horse tensed. "From up ahead!"

The footmen pulled back, crowding the nervous horse as the footsteps grew nearer. A tall, dark man emerged from the foliage ahead. He cocked his head to the side, curiously surveying the scene before him. Upon his black breastplate, the chimera glittered golden and red. The cowled figure slid from the saddle and pushed his way through the footmen to kneel before the stranger.

"I am your most humble servant, my lord," he murmured, reverently. "It was I that sent the girl to free you."

"Truly? Then, you shall be well rewarded. But, where is my lovely, now?" the Chimera asked. The figure lifted its head and pushed back the hood. The watery almost colorless eyes studied the Chimera for a long moment. The wind tussled the thinning strands on top of his round head, revealing the shiny pink scalp beneath. His thin lips pulled back in a nervous smile.

"I do not know, lord. I never met her, only her brother. But, I think they are still in the town. Please, allow me to lead you to my home, where you may recuperate." The man gestured behind him to the horse.

"Your beast will not carry me," the Chimera said simply, as though speaking to an idiot. He crooked his finger at the cowering footmen. "But, they will serve, nicely."

The men began to scream, dropping to their knees in pain. They tore at their hair, crawling over each other in the maddening attempt to get away. Their bodies began to meld, muscles splitting skin and hair growing long and shaggy. Bones sprouted from flesh, elongating, and cracking. The cowled figure began to retch and turned away. When he looked back scant seconds later a large black horse stood on the spot where the men had fallen, its eyes pools of liquid dark. It snorted, tossing a glorious mane of silken hair in invitation. The Chimera strode to its' side and, grabbing a handful of its' lustrous mane, swung onto its' back. The horse reared, kicking its' forelocks high and then settled regally. "What is your name, servant?"

"Hume, my lord," the man mounted his horse and waited. The Chimera nodded.

"What do you wait for, Hume? Lead on," he ordered.

The Chimera strode through the hall of Hume's spacious home, nose wrinkled in disgust. How utterly tacky this man's sense of style was. Gaudy pieces of painted statuary littered every nook and crevice in the opulent three story home with its open garden courtyard in the center. He looked up at the top floor balcony and stopped. A young woman stood there, hiding behind a column, watching him. He smiled invitingly, gesturing to her to join him. She darted away from the balcony to the shadowy recesses of the inside. He growled. That was the second time a mere girl had dared defy him. This time, the slight would not go unpunished. He took a step, rising through the air and setting his foot down on the balcony rail, then dropped gracefully to the floor. Her path burned before him like a firelight trail and he stalked his prey through the upstairs chambers. On the main stairwell he caught her by the arm and she let out a startled little shriek, looking up at him with fear clouded eyes.

"When your master tells you to come, you obey," he snarled, twisting her arm savagely. She cried out again and his hand cracked across her face. She lost her balance and he let go of her arm, watching in amusement as she tumbled down the marble curving stairs. She screamed, long and terrified, until her neck snapped somewhere near the second floor. Hume came running through the garden, his thin hair flying in wisps, his robe flapping. To the Chimera, he looked like an emaciated old bird trying to fly. Hume reached the bottom of the stairs seconds before the girl's body and she landed at his feet with a heavy thud. He sank to his knees howling like an animal and cradled the dead girl in his arms. The Chimera walked leisurely down the steps and stopped on the last one to look down at the blubbering man. Hume glared up at him.

"Why?" he demanded raggedly. "Why did you do this?"

"She needed to be taught obedience. You are too lenient with your slaves," Chimera growled.

"She was my daughter! My baby! The apple of my eye!" Hume sobbed.

"Then, I have spared you the pain of seeing her spoilt and thankless."

"Please, my lord. Please," Hume begged. The Chimera let out an irritated sigh, and then held out his hand over the girl's body. Nothing happened. Hume eased her body to the ground and shot to his feet, hands clenched in rage. "Damn you! I brought you back from the dead and this is how you repay me? By slaying the light of my life?"

"Father?" a small voice asked from his feet. The girl looked up at him with confused eyes. "Why are you shouting?"

"Velka! Velka, my love!" he cried, dropping to his knees once more. He hugged her tightly to his chest.

"You had better remember who serves whom, Hume," the Chimera growled menacingly. "I do not take being spoken to that way lightly and do not think that I am your puppet to command. I am the Chimera and I will be revered."

The Chimera stepped over them and walked back through the garden. A wicked smile crossed his handsome face. Behind him, Velka began to scream.

Kari splashed water on her face. The stream was clear and cold, swollen with run off from the last melting snows. She ran a wet hand across her neck and dribbled water down her chest. Where were those two? She stood up and looked around. The bank was clear for a handful of feet before the trees started pressing in. The horses stood a little off, drinking from the stream and munching sweet grass. But, there were no signs of the boys. She removed her headband and dunked her head into the stream, held it there as long as she could stand the cold, and then flipped it back over her shoulders. The deep auburn darkened to a rich black as it slapped her back, and she deftly plaited it before tying it in place with the braided leather of her headband.

"Little lovely! I command you to come to me!" a voice boomed from the trees. Kari jumped, nearly falling into the stream. She heard their giggles before she saw them, leaning on each other just inside the tree line. "Did you see her jump?"

"That was priceless!" Jackie whooped, wiping a tear from his eye. "I've never seen your sister so skittish, Malcolm!"

"Good thing it doesn't run in the family," Malcolm agreed.

"Very funny. Hey, your village sent word, they want their idiots back," she snapped. She bent and began packing up the meager remains of their breakfast. Their luck had held, and they had bought a loaf of bread and a wedge of cheese from a passing farmer on his way into town. She wrapped it carefully and stuck it into Jackie's pack.

"Ow, come on, Kari. We were only joking," Jackie reached for her arm and she jerked away.

"That scared me, okay? Not you idiots; that whole thing back there. I just want to get as far away as I can and forget it happened," she snapped peevishly, hoisting the pack onto her shoulder.

"I'm sorry, Kari. I didn't realize," Jackie reached for the pack and she reluctantly gave it up. "Something else bothering you?"

"I just have one of my bad feelings, that's all," she shrugged. "Let's get going, okay?"

"Sure. We'll be in Havildadt in three more days. We can have a proper meal and rest there. Check out the ins and outs of the inns along the way," Malcolm grinned goofily at his own joke and Kari gave him a grudging smile.

"I can't believe we've been on the road for three days already," she groaned. She stuck her foot in the stirrup and drug herself onto the saddle. "My butt is so sore."

"Better your butt than your feet," Malcolm commented dryly. They rode in silence for a long while, watching the foliage pass by in the dreamy warmth of the young spring day. Dewdrops added diamond sparkles to the new green buds surrounding them. After a few miles, Kari sighed.

"Do you really think that was an illusion?" she hazarded, timidly. Malcolm scoffed.

"You think we really woke up a seven hundred year old dead guy?"

"I don't know. The Chimera was supposed to be an evil wizard, why couldn't he come back from the dead?" she shrugged.

"Because, the Chimera was a legend to frighten children," Jackie insisted. "Nothing more."

"But..."

"But nothing, Kari. Now, forget about it. Let's just enjoy the ride to Havildadt." They rode all day, only Jackie breaking the silence every now and again as he broke into one old song or another. Kari kept her eyes forward watching the horizon for signs of trouble, but every instinct in her screamed for her to turn around and look back. Look back toward Jencarta from where they had come.

Chapter Three

The ground heaved mightily, separating under the strain of pressure from within. Arms stabbed upward from the sucking soil, pulling tattered torsos from the graves, spewing skeletons out of the earth. They lurched toward him, forming into ragged lines. Chimera watched them coolly from his horse as they arrayed themselves before him, a legion of the damned ready for inspection. He inclined his head and they marched into the trees, heading for Jencarta. He followed at a regal pace, a cowled Hume limping along at his side as his army tore through the undergrowth, eyes glowing green with malice. The lines spread out in a curving arc, circling around the village. Chimera nodded and Hume raised a horn to his lips. The clear sound of the horn resounded in the early morning air. The army surged forward. Terrified screams filled the morning.

"What lovely music, don't you think?" Chimera asked Hume. Hume shuddered. In moments it was over and the survivors were rounded up and brought before the Chimera. He surveyed the faces of the young men and women, most barely out of childhood and he held up a hand for their attention. "I am the Chimera. You were spared for various reasons, but I assure you that I can and will slay you at the change of the breeze. Now, you have a castle to rebuild."

He motioned and the army started off, herding the sniffling and battered survivors into the forest. "Hume," he snapped. Hume's flayed hand grasped the mane of the horse, and he raised his skinless face to his master. The meat of his face steamed in the sunlight, his lidless eyes flashing in pain.

"My Master, what would you have me do?" he asked, solicitously. Chimera looked down at him, disdainfully and twitched his horse away.

"Fetch your skin from your house and a quill. I have messages to write."

Kari set another tankard of ale down in front of the customer, a ragged looking traveler who had come in late the night before. His bowed face was covered by wild grey hair, but his trembling hands were young. She scooped up the coin he laid on the table and turned to go.

"It's the end of humanity, you know?" he said, suddenly. She turned back to him with a smile.

"I'll admit, it's not palace fare, but the ale's not that bad," she joked. He raised his haunted eyes to hers and the smile died on her lips.

"The dead walk in the north. They prey upon the living. The Chimera has returned," he downed the ale, slamming the cup on the table. She stood mesmerized by his desolate voice, and he took her wrist, pulling her close. "There is a squad of the undead that he is teaching to ride winged wereleopards. He calls them the Hunt. And that's what they do. They hunt humans, carry them off. It's not safe to go outside after dark. That's when they come. You can hear the wind moaning in terror as they ride. If you hear that moaning, girl, you get inside and you bolt the doors and windows, fast."

"Why are you telling me this?" she breathed. A tear slid down his cheek.

"You remind me of my sweet little sister, Sara. I couldn't save her, maybe I can save you," he sighed, releasing her wrist. He dropped several more coins on the table and rose. "His army is sweeping this way, down from Jencarta. You would do well to spread the word. Better yet, get yourself on a ship and leave this godforsaken land like me."

He limped out of the common room, closing the front doors firmly behind him against the stifling heat of late summer. Kari looked around at the small common room. They had bought themselves a dive down by the waterfront and managed to fix it up into something almost reputable. It was all she had ever wanted: a secure home and living. She loved cleaning up and serving guests; even cooking was a joy. No more back alley break-ins, or market day pocket slashings to feed her. She was finally going to be legit. And they still had money left over for the lean times. They were set, everything bought and paid for.

With the blood of others.

"Malcolm!" she cried, running through the kitchen and into the back yard. He bent over the washtub, bronze back bare and rippling as he stirred the boiling kettle. "Malcolm!"

"I'm almost done, Kari, give me a break!" he snapped, peevishly. She grabbed his arm and spun him around. "Curse it, Kari...What's wrong?"

"The Chimera," she gasped.

"I told you, Kari, that was an illusion," he groaned.

"No! Someone just told me, he's back! He has an army and they are coming this way. He has a Hunt, they fly and they carry people off and..."

"And whoever told you this is laughing his ass off because you believed his wild nightmare. Honestly, little sister, you used to be so skeptical, now you just believe anything. Now, go on back inside and let me finish this. Scoot," he turned her around and popped her on the rear. She glared over her shoulder at him, but did as she was told. Malcolm went back to stirring the sheets, chewing his lower lip. He and Jackie had tried so hard to keep her from hearing the rumors from the north. They knew how much they would upset her. Jackie had been to the Thieves' Guild several times, asking for news from the northern regions. It was never good. They hoped that the winter would be a hard one, like last year, and the northern passages would freeze, making travel impossible for the oncoming horde. Malcolm doubted it. What hardships did the dead fear, anyway?

Jackie came around the side of the building, his usually jocular face pale and serious. He threw himself down on the ground beside the pot and absently added a stick to the hungry flames. He sat there in silence for a long time, watching the flames lick the black bottom of the cauldron, then looked up at Malcolm with watery eyes.

"The last message from the north," he began. He swallowed hard, and then tried again. "The last message from the north is that the capital city is surrounded by the walking dead. Every time a man falls inside to enemy weapons, he rises up and attacks his comrades. The king has locked himself in his royal apartments and surrounded himself with all available guards. They don't expect him to make it out alive. The Chimera. Oh, gods, Malcolm. We really did wake the Chimera. And he's going to turn his eyes this way!"

"Keep your calm, Jackie. Kari knows about the army, but not how bad it is. And we don't want her to know, right?" Malcolm used a pole to tip the cauldron. Its' contents splashed onto a wooden lattice secured several inches over a gravel filled channel that led to the edge of the cliff far behind the stables. There the water plummeted several hundred feet to the ocean below.

"Right," Jackie agreed firmly. "But, how do we keep it from her? As soon as he takes over the kingdom, he will send his legions to secure the south."

"We have to leave," Malcolm growled. Using the pole to press water from the sheets. "We'll sell the inn; it's actually worth something now. And we'll get ourselves passage on the next ship out of here. Go further south. Maybe to an island."

"And how will we explain it to Kari?" Jackie demanded.

"We'll tell her that one of us was recognized by the authorities. She won't argue with that," Malcolm leaned on the pole and rubbed his eyes. Why couldn't the fates just once give him a break? Jackie nodded.

"Mackenzie. He's been after us to buy the place back. I'll go see him, double the price, and then I'll go to the harbor. You tell Kari." He disappeared around the side of the building. Malcolm sighed, and then turned to go in. Kari stood in the open doorway staring at him.

"I'll start packing," she said, simply, and turned back inside.

The Chimera rode up to the iron gates of the city, his tunic of black and gold flashing in the shimmering heat of the afternoon sun. He raised his hands dramatically over his head and called up to the cowering people on the battlements.

"I grow weary of this game. I give you this final chance. Open the gate and you will live. If I must open the gate, you will all surely die."

After a moments silence, the gate mechanism began to grind and squeal, and the iron gate parted before swinging slowly backward. Chimera and his army advanced through the streets, heading directly for the multi-spired castle at the city's heart. People ran, screaming from the skeletal warriors, hiding from the cruel green eyes that seemed to see everything and nothing inside those dead faces. The Chimera rode at the crest of the wave, his stallion crushing holes in the ground wherever its mighty hooves thundered down.

Inside the castle, women huddled in fear, clutching children close. The king paced his throne room, pausing every now and again as if listening. The steward rushed in, panic stricken, and fell to his knees before the king.

"They are inside the gates, my lord. He rides at the very head of the army! What shall we do?" he cried. The king placed a comforting hand on his shoulder.

"I shall meet him here in the throne room, Gregory. And I shall die with dignity. But, I am not dead, yet, and you are still sworn to me." The king pulled his old friend to his feet. "Listen closely, Gregory. Draw on your fearlessness from better days past. You must lead all those you can through the secret tunnels. Make for the southern cities. Find Michael, my son, and tell him that his birthright has been stolen. He must gather his people and fight. He will know what to do. Now, go," Gregory nodded, and ran for the door, yelling orders. "Gregory!"

"Yes, my lord?" he asked, turning back. The king stood frozen for a moment and then swallowed hard.

"Tell my boy, my son, that his father loved him very much."

Gregory nodded and then slipped out the door. The king squared his shoulders and walked back to the throne, settling himself with great dignity. He waited, the sounds of running feet beating in time to his erratic heart. From below came the sounds of gigantic hammers blasting the oak gates. They held for a handful of heartbeats and then splintered. Shrieks echoed through the corridors and the sounds of hooves mounting the stairs shocked him into action. He snatched up the sword that rested beside the throne and stood defiantly facing the half open door. The sound of heavy, snorted breaths rung down the hall and the slow sound of hoof beats grew closer. A huge black beast nosed its' way through the door, its' hooves striking sparks off the polished floor. The Chimera rode leisurely into the throne room, his eyes fixed on the defiant king.

"And who will you hide behind, now?" he demanded. The king raised his chin.

"I hide from neither man nor beast. Nor Hell spawn!" he spat. The Chimera raised an eyebrow. The sword in the king's hand began to shift. The blade suddenly shot backward, piercing his throat with vipers' teeth. In horror, the king let go of the snakes tail and clutched at its' fanged mouth. The tail whipped around his neck and chest and began to squeeze. The king struggled, his face a mottled purple, his tongue rolling out of blue lips. His eyes bulged and he made a desperate, gasping sound and then fell forward onto the floor. The Chimera watched as the snake uncoiled and began to swallow the body.

"And so shall I swallow the world," he assured the horse, patting its' neck.

Chapter Four

Jackie returned after dark, looking tired and depressed. He slid behind the bar and began helping Malcolm serve drinks.

"He won't have the funds for a solid week, and the quickest passage I could book is in two weeks," he growled. Malcolm scooped coins off the counter and set down another tankard.

"It'll have to do."

"Did you tell Kari?"

"She overheard. Hasn't said much, though, but she's got us ready to move out."

"Always was the efficient one," Jackie commented, watching Kari wade through the bustling tables, tray held high overhead. She was laughing at something or someone. His heart clenched. "She deserves better."

"That's why we left Grams. Remember? To make a better life than prostitute or thief for Kari? And we will. As soon as we get to the islands, my little sister will be queen of her own domain," Malcolm vowed, refilling another tankard. Kari turned, catching Jackie's eye, and smiled. Slightly sad and wistful under the facade, it broke his heart as surely as a stone through glass. She disappeared back into the kitchen for more food.

"I don't think she'd be happy as a queen. Just as long as she was free to do as she pleased," Jackie sighed, wiping his hands on a rag. Just then, the doors burst inward and a ragged looking young boy came charging in.

"The king is dead! The king is dead and his city fallen!" he screamed at the top of his lungs. "The Chimera has taken the throne!" The common room burst into a panic, people rushing to escape into the night, crushing friends and neighbors in the surge toward the door. The messenger fell beneath their trampling feet, and Jackie vaulted the bar, slicing through the crowd like a knife through hard bread. He lifted the boy over his head and pressed his back against the wall, watching the fleeing mob. Kari ran from the kitchen and Malcolm pulled her to his side. In moments, the crowd was gone, leaving a handful of people crushed on the stone floor. Jackie carried the boy over to the bar and laid him down on it.

"Oh, gods, Jackie, is he alive?" Kari demanded, her eyes filling with tears. Jackie pressed an ear to the boy's chest.

"There's a faint heartbeat. Malcolm, get him some brandy," Jackie urged. Malcolm disappeared into the back. Kari dipped a cloth into a pitcher of water and began mopping the boy's forehead with it. Her eyes strayed to the figures lying broken on the floor.

"Jackie?" she whispered, imploringly. He nodded, squeezing her hand gently before going to check on the others. She wept silently as he moved from one to the other, pressing his ear against chest and back. He looked up from the last one and caught her eye, shook his head. The boy coughed, his eyelids fluttering and suddenly Malcolm was there with a tankard of brandy. Kari raised the boy and supported him while Malcolm pressed the cup to his lips. The boy coughed and sputtered as the liquid burned down his throat and his eyes shot open.

"The Chimera!" he gasped, tensing to bolt.

"Easy, little one. He will not get you, here," Kari assured him, holding him firmly against her chest.

"But, I must warn the people!" he shouted, struggling to rise. Malcolm raised the boys face to meet his eyes.

"You did, lad. You did. Don't you hear?" he asked, gently. Outside in the streets, the town bells were ringing and people rushed through the streets, shouting and screaming. "If you try to go out there now, you'll be crushed, and that will make your parents very sad."

"My parents are dead. The Chimera's soldiers killed them!" the boy choked. "What do I care to die?"

"Because, your parents would have wanted you to live," Kari said softly.

"And you can't take vengeance if you are dead," Malcolm growled. The boy glared up at him, his eyes defiant despite the sheen of tears.

"What do you care?" he demanded. "Why would a stranger matter to you?"

"Because we know what it's like to be alone in the world," Jackie sighed.

"What's your name?" Kari asked, gently, and he turned his head to look at her.

"Jonah."

"Well, Jonah, I am Kari, and that is Jackie, and that is Malcolm. And now, we are not strangers anymore," she smiled, wiping a stray tear from the corner of his eye. "And we will take care of each other, like a family."

"Tell me, Jonah, how did you come to find out about the king?" Malcolm asked, pressing the tankard into the boy's palms. Jonah gulped the brandy and shuddered.

"My father was a woodsman, keeping tend over the animals in the king's hunting arena. People from the castle came, fleeing in terror into the woods where we lived. They screamed the news. Father recognized one, the royal steward. He paused long enough to tell father that he must seek out the Prince and tell him the king was dead. Then, he screamed at father to run and spread the news. The Chimera had taken the throne!"" Jonah drained the tankard, wiping his mouth with the back of his hand. "The soldiers broke through the trees then and....and...oh, Gods!"

Kari turned the boy and cradled him against her chest as he dissolved into tears. She mouthed the words 'More brandy' at Malcolm and he hurried away. When he returned, Kari was rocking Jonah, stroking his hair as he sobbed. Malcolm refilled the tankard. Jackie nodded toward the bodies on the floor and Malcolm followed him over to them. Grimly, they moved them to the wall next to the door and covered them with tablecloths, the soft sound of Kari's crooning moving them to be gentle. When they were finished, they returned to the bar where Jonah hiccupped against her chest.

"Can you go on?" Jackie asked him. Jonah looked up at Kari pleadingly.

"You don't have to if you don't want, Jonah," she assured him, pushing the hair from his soaked forehead. "It might help to talk about it, but you do not have to." Jonah nodded, taking a deep and quivering breath. He leaned his head against her breast and closed his eyes.

"A heartbeat after the steward told us to run, they broke through the trees. Tall, huge men on black horses with red eyes. They were dressed in black armor, with gold crests on the breastplate. Some sort of lion-dragon thing. I don't know. They wore no helms, and that was the scariest part: Because they were corpses. Skeletons wielding long swords with curved blades. Some of them didn't have jaws. Others were just decayed faces, with worms crawling in and out. But, their eyes were alive, flickering green and black." Jonah paused to take another drink, and his voice started to become dreamy. "I was frozen with fear as one rode straight at me, his sword raised to slice my head clean off. I heard my mother scream no, and suddenly she was in front of me, and the blade was in her neck. Her body fell on top of me and I blacked out. When I woke, I pushed her off and looked around. Bodies lay scattered everywhere, and the house was on fire. I found my father lying near the house. He wasn't dead. He..."

"Jonah, you don't have to go on," Malcolm said as the boy faltered. Jonah opened his eyes and looked up into Malcolm's.

"Warn the people, Jonah, he said. Warn the people and find the prince. Only he can stop the Chimera. Go, my son. I am sorry you are all alone, now," Jonah sobbed. Kari tightened her arms around him.

"You are not alone, Jonah. And you have made your father proud. You did exactly what he told you to do. I'm going to put you to bed, now, and I want you to rest," Kari told him, easing him off the bar. He clutched her arms, terror making his face a pale mask.

"Don't leave me!" he cried. She smiled, reassuringly.

"I will be right next door to you, and I will come if you call me. I promise. Let's go." Kari walked him slowly from the room and up the stairs. Malcolm looked at Jackie's stricken face.

"How do we make this right?" Jackie whispered. "How?"

"By finding the prince."

"And then what?"

"Joining his army. We will put Kari and Jonah on the boat to the islands and then we will take up the fight against the Chimera. We will right this wrong we are responsible for, Jackie. Somehow," Malcolm vowed.

Chapter Five

Gregory stumbled through the streets of Violet, his royal robes of stewardship tattered and covered with filth. His silver hair was matted with filth and leaves, and he muttered to himself as he staggered along. Dead. All who had followed him were dead. If he had not fallen into a muddy ravine and been overlooked, he would be dead, too. He still must fulfill his liege's last command. Somewhere in this small town, Prince Michael was enjoying his last moments of peace and happiness. Gregory had to find him. He stumbled over a paving stone and fell heavily to the ground, smashing his chin. Blood filled his mouth and he spat violently into the trickle of water running alongside the street. Light spilled suddenly from an opening door, and the sounds of laughter echoed through the deserted lane.

"What's this? Disgusting! The night watch should be ashamed!" a female voice dripping with scorn exclaimed over his head. "I thought all derelicts were run out of town!"

"If they are, then more's the shame on your city, Madam," another, younger and more masculine voice snapped. Strong hands seized Gregory gently under the arms and lifted him to his feet. "There you are, sir. May I be of some assistance to you?" Gregory raised his eyes to thank the young man and gasped.

"Oh, the Gods be Praised!" he shouted, throwing his arms around the prince. Michael stood stunned for a moment, then pried him loose and held him at arms length, studying him in the light from the still opened door.

"Gregory? Is that you? By the Gods, what has happened? Tell me, Gregory!" he demanded, urgently. Tears streamed down Gregory's dirty face as he stared at Michael.

"Your father is murdered, the city thrown down. The Chimera has taken the throne," he wailed.

"The Chimera is a myth, Gregory. You are stunned," Michael insisted, sliding his arm beneath the older man's shoulder. "We will get you to the inn and get you cleaned up. No doubt food and a little rest will help you collect yourself." Gregory shoved him away and then grasped his arms desperately.

"No, there had been rumors that he had arisen, again. He is alive, Michael! And he sends his undead soldiers after you. We must get you someplace safe so that you can gather your army." Gregory spat another wad of blood from his mouth. "Michael, please, you must believe me!"

"I do, Gregory. Still, let us get you to the inn, and when you have had a little rest, we will decide what must be done. Madam?" Michael turned to the young lady and two other men that were accompanying him. "I beg your pardon, and I thank you for your excellent company this eve. My guard will escort you home. Good night." Michael didn't wait for a response from the pale young woman, simply turned and began walking, pulling Gregory firmly with him. His mind reeled as they traveled the dark streets of the town to the well-lit inn at its edge. Gregory suddenly stopped, and grabbed Michael's wrist.

"I have a message from your father."

"It can wait."

"No. He said tell my boy, my son, that his father loved him very much."

Michael raised his eyes to the overcast sky above him and wept.

Chapter Six

Hume stood, trembling outside the doors to the throne room. A breeze blew through the hall, sending a shiver along the raw muscles of his face and hands. Needles tingled along his flayed flesh as he pulled the cowl tight around his ravaged face.

"What do you wait for, Hume?" the Chimera inquired from inside the throne room. Hume squared his shoulders and entered to kneel at the foot of the new throne. Formed from obsidian, the lion skull roared silently at the chamber, emerald flames flickering in empty eye sockets, and sitting in the open jaw, the Chimera gazed disdainfully down at the quivering man at his feet. "You thought to control me? How pathetic. What do you have to report, slave?"

"My lord, the city is taken, and the soldiers have returned to report all the escapees slain. I have searched all the bodies myself, my lord…"

"And?"

"And there is no sign of the prince," Hume whispered. The booted foot lashed out, catching him across the face and sending him sprawling. The cold stone of the floor seared against his exposed muscles and tissues, and Hume screamed in pain, scrambling to his feet.

"Imbecile!" Chimera roared. "I will find him myself!"

He stormed behind the throne to a hidden stairwell and climbed the steep winding steps. He passed several doors, but kept ascending. Finally, the stairs ended at a simple wooden door and he pushed it open, stepping out into the night. Brilliant stars illuminated the balcony on which he stood, wrapped around the tallest spire in the castle. He raised his arms to the night, his head thrown back, words spilling from his lips in a vicious guttural tongue that had not been uttered in centuries. In the streets below, people wailed in new terror as the ground beneath them heaved, spewing up decayed bodies to a new and hideously unnatural life.

"Rise! Rise! From the pits of Hell, I summon thee. Rise! From the rings of purgatory, from the foundations of earth, I call you!" he intoned, darkly. The bodies lurched to attention as fleshlings ran to hide in their homes. "Hear your master's voice, all along the continent, rise and show no mercy! Bring me the whelp of the dead king! Crush all those that stand against you, tear flesh from bone, crush muscle and sinew. Live, my children! Live!" The Chimera dropped his arms and stepped back inside, descending the steps with a slight skip. Waiting for him at the foot of the throne, a squad of twenty undead soldiers knelt patiently in a line, their heads lowered. Chimera smiled at the tattered patch sewn to their tunics. The emblem of the mighty lion headed dragon, the chimera itself. "How long we have waited, Dorgath. Rise, my faithful hunters!"

They rose swiftly and silently to their feet, clicking their booted heels in attention.

"Master," their leader hissed through dislocated jaw, nodding his head in respect. "Your Hunt awaits its' first command to serve."

"Raise your werebeasts, men. The Hunt will ride, soon. Until then, take what pleasure you wish, even claim flesh for yourselves if you so desire. There are so many here who are not only wastes of flesh, but they have an abundance of flesh to spare," Chimera laughed. The squad of twenty corpses banged their right wrists against their chests, brushing fingers over the patches each time. The leader, Dorgath, grinned maliciously and bowed.

"Thank you, my lord. Your indulgence is sweet," he hissed. Chimera sat down on the throne once more, waving his hand dismissively as he did so. The squad spun on their heels and marched from the room. Hume detached himself from the wall curtains and sidled over to the throne.

"My lord," he hazarded, "what pleasures did you speak of?"

"The same pleasures all men partake of, Hume. Even the dead hunger." Chimera said simply. From the corridors, frightened screams began to echo through the castle.

Chapter Seven

Jackie stalked grimly through the common room, his jaw clenched tightly. Business had resumed in the week since Jonah's arrival, but the room was still over half empty. That wasn't his present concern, though. Jonah set two tankards on Kari's tray, and she tussled his hair before carrying it off. Jonah smiled after her and began wiping down the counter.

"Hey, little man, where is Malcolm?" Jackie asked, forcing a smile. Jonah looked up and grinned.

"In the kitchen."

"You're doing a great job, little man," Jackie winked before disappearing through the kitchen doors. Malcolm stood before the stew kettle, stripped to the waste and sweating as he stirred. "We've got problems."

"What now?" Malcolm grunted. Jackie picked up the knife on the table and began cutting one of the many peeled potatoes that lay piled beside it.

"Mackenzie. He's gone. Packed up his house and split. We've no one to buy the place from us."

"And with no funds, we can't put Kari and Jonah on the boat," Malcolm growled.

"Even if we had funds, the boats have deserted the harbor. There isn't even a scow or fishing boat to be seen anywhere along the horizon." Jackie slid the pieces away and picked up another potato. "What are we gonna do, Mal?"

"What about the horses? Are they still in the stable?" Malcolm asked, rubbing his eyes, tiredly.

"I believe so. Alcady has the stable locked up tighter than a crab's ass. What are you thinking?" Jackie demanded. "We can't ride them over the water."

"I don't know, Jackie. I don't know what to do," Malcolm sighed. He stirred the bubbling pot in silence for a long while, until Jackie moved to dump the sliced potatoes into it. "What if we send Kari and Jonah west along the coast? The boats have to dock somewhere. Isn't there a peninsula somewhere along the bottom of this godsforsaken kingdom that leads further south?"

"I think. Would they be safe traveling alone, though?" Jackie chewed his lower lip.

"Here's what we will do, Jackie. Screw the inn. We'll take what money we have, and what food we can carry, get the horses and find the peninsula. We'll get Kari and Jonah to safety, and then we will find the prince and join up with him," Malcolm stirred furiously as the pot began to bubble once more. "Why does she insist on stew on such a hot day?"

"You know how she is about hot meals," Jackie shrugged. "Here, I'll stir for a while, you rest." Jackie took the paddle from him. Malcolm went outside into the cooler air of the yard and splashed water from the rain barrel on his face. He gazed out over the yard and listened to the pounding surf below, and his heart clenched. He didn't want to give this up; it was all he had ever dreamed of, all he had ever worked for. His conscience pricked him viciously: to attain this, he had turned loose a monster on the world, a monster that would take it away again, anyway. Better to give it up than have it stolen. He hoped that Kari would see it the same way. She asked for so little from him, from life, and she gave so much in return. Look at the way she had taken to caring for

Jonah. She treated him like a son, and the boy followed her like a puppy. Malcolm shook himself, hardening his resolve. He picked a shirt up from the drying screen and put it on. "Jackie!"

"Yeah?" Jackie poked his head out the door.

"I'm going to see Alcady."

"Right. Don't let him tell you we owe. Kari pays for the whole month at the beginning each time." Jackie warned, and then popped back inside. Jonah stood inside the doors to the common room, holding a tray stacked with dishes. He blinked, and then moved to put them in the sink.

"Who's Alcady?" he asked softly as Jackie went back to stirring the stew.

"He runs the town stable. Are there many people out there still?" Jackie asked. Jonah shook his head. "Good. Go get Kari for me; I need to talk to you both."

Chapter Eight

Chimera gazed intently at the gathered werebeasts. Twenty cat like bodies rippled with muscles underneath sleek ebony flesh, fangs of pearl glimmered in the waning light of the afternoon. Eyes of red glowed from beneath pointed ears, and the sharp claws of their feet dug mercilessly into the ground, tearing out large clods of earth. They prowled restlessly before him. Dorgath walked up behind the Chimera and cleared his throat.

"You sent for me, my lord?" he asked. Chimera turned. Dorgath's skeletal face was covered by smooth skin, stretched thinly. It gave him an even more horrifying appearance than had the decay. Chimera nodded approvingly, noting that Dorgath's hands and arms were still without skin. Noticing his questioning glance, Dorgath smiled. "I enjoy the feel of my weapons, sire. Flesh only gets in the way."

"Very good. Are you and your men ready?"

"Yes, sire. What do we seek?"

"A girl, Dorgath. I owe her a very special debt. Take my hand." Chimera held out his palm, and Dorgath closed his meaty fingers around it. Immediately, the picture from the tomb flashed across his eyes, and the form of a girl burned itself into his memory. "Hume believes they are in the south. Find her. Kill whomever you like, flay the men if they are with her. Bring them over to join your Hunt if you wish, but bring me the girl unspoilt."

"Yes, my lord," Dorgath released his hand and waved. The other squad members mounted the beasts. At his whistle, the werebeasts unfurled great wings from their sleek sides and sprang into the air. Chimera watched them until they were mere specks on the horizon, absently rubbing his chest.

"Soon, my little Kari. Soon."

Michael stroked his mount's withers, frowning into the overcast sky. His mind turned over the latest news from the north as they rode, a silent quartet among the lush foliage of the south: Squads of the dead, torn from the earth to roam the lands, searching for him. Luckily, the dead still rested for the time here in the south. A good omen, that. The Chimera's powers were not absolute. Not yet. There had been no word from the capital city; he would have to try to contact her. Hopefully, she still lived. That was the cornerstone of the pitiful plan he was forming. Her survival. A king needed information to form a successful campaign, after all, and she knew everything.

"My liege," Gregory hazarded, timidly. Michael pulled himself back to the present and turned in the saddle to look behind. "How much farther is the Ichthus Peninsula? I have all but lost my bearings out here," he whined. Michael took a deep breath, reminding himself that this was one of his father's friends, a great warrior in his own time: now gone to seed and whining, mind you, but he was still deserving of respect.

"A few hundred leagues. Don't worry, Gregory. Just a day or so more and we will reach Havildadt where we can rest, possibly even charter a boat to take us the rest of the way. Have patience," he said, turning to look ahead again. Ahead of him, Max slowed his pace and dropped back to ride beside Michael.

"My lord, something troubles me. I can't say what it is, but something doesn't feel right," he growled. Michael nodded.

"I feel it, too, Max. Where are all the forest noises? Be alert, my friend."

"Killian, keep your eyes peeled," Max called to the younger knight where he rode beside Gregory.

"I thought I might take a long nap," Killian sneered, and Max rolled his eyes.

"Those two are well matched. Youths folly and old ages complaints," Michael sighed. He turned in his saddle to rebuke the young knight. With a crash, bodies flung themselves from the trees, swinging bright weapons. A sword, long and curved slashed through the air, sending Gregory's head flying from his torso. Their horses screamed, rearing back from the decayed hands that groped blindly for the reigns. Michael shouted hoarsely in revulsion, swinging his sword in deadly arcs, slicing the lurching corpses in two. Killian shouted in panic, and Michael looked up in time to see the younger man tumble from his horse and be swarmed by the undead. Michael leapt from the saddle, clearing the beasts away to pull Killian to his feet.

"My Lord!" Max shouted in warning and Michael spun. The sword slipped past his guard and sank into his shoulder. The decayed face leered at him for a long second before the undead pulled the sword from his shoulder and moved to deliver a killing blow. Max's shout heralded salvation as his blade sliced the creatures arm off, then arced back to slice the surprised head from its' torso. Michael sank to the ground, blood pouring from his wound, and darkness claimed him. The last thing he saw was the tide of undead rushing forward to swarm him.

Malcolm returned later with the horses in tow and a few coins in his pouch. Alcady had grudgingly refunded the rest of the payment that Kari had made. Of course, Malcolm had had to remind him of what faithful and prompt customers they had been. Malcolm shook his head, leading the horses through the mostly deserted streets. The sun was setting and most people were already locked inside their homes, cowering against the sounds of the night. How pathetic. The Chimera and his forces had not even arrived yet and already the town lived like it was under siege. Those that had remained had gathered tribute and sent it northward in hopes that their meager bribe would keep the Chimera at bay. Malcolm had contributed nothing to the collection, silently figuring that giving life to the beast was enough. The rest had fled the town with whatever they could carry. Malcolm turned the horses onto the side street where the inn was located.

A single lamp burned beneath the inn sign, illuminating the green swan painted on the board. Jackie had wanted to dub the place the Palace of the Seasick Swan. Kari had refused that idea from the start. Malcolm smiled, remembering the argument. She had eventually won, naming the place the Emerald Swan. Home. The only real home any of them had ever had. How he would miss it. He tied the horses to the rail post beside the entrance and pushed the door open. The common room was silent and dim, only two lamps burning on either side of the kitchen door. The place felt oddly empty, foreign.

"Kari? Jackie? Jonah?" he called, weakly, his mouth and throat suddenly dry. A pan dropped somewhere in the kitchen and the doors swung open. Kari walked in, wearing her old brown tunic and breeches, a cloak gathered in her arms. She sighed in relief when she caught sight of him.

"Where have you been? We were beginning to worry," she snapped harshly, and then her tone softened. "I'm sorry, Malcolm. Did you get the horses?"

"They're outside."

"We're almost finished packing up. We decided to use mine as a packhorse, and double up on the others. Come help me bring this stuff out," she ordered, dumping her cloak on the bar. He followed her into the kitchen, whistling sharply at the pile of neatly packed gear. Without a word, she began stacking his arms full of parcels.

"How did you know?"

"Jackie."

"Uhm." The doors into the common room burst open, and there was shouting. Malcolm dropped the bundles and he and Kari raced into the common room. Two men were laying a third on one of the tables. Covered in blood and dirt, they shouted for the innkeeper as they began to strip their friend. "What's going on here?"

"This is your liege, Prince Michael, and he is gravely wounded. Fetch a healer, peasant, now!" the younger of the men barked. Kari pushed him aside and looked down at the pale young man on the table. His face was set in a grimace and blood soaked his shirt. She pulled the small knife she always carried in her belt and began cutting away the blood soaked cloth.

"The healer ran at first sound of the king's death, and watch your tone with my brother or find yourself out in the damn street," she snarled. "You are on borrowed time if this is who you claim, and you'd do best to remember not to make enemies unnecessarily!"

"What's the commotion?" Jackie demanded, coming into the room with a long knife, Jonah trailing behind.

"We've got wounded here, Jackie. I need hot water. Jonah, run and fetch me any linens we didn't pack. Hurry, now, both of you," Kari snapped. She uncovered a deep wound in the man's left shoulder and groaned. "No time for boiling, got to stop the blood. Malcolm, your tunic." He stripped it off and handed it to her, and she folded it deftly and pressed it to the hole. The two men backed away from the table.

"What happened?" Malcolm demanded of the older of the two.

"We were traveling from Violet, heading toward the Ichthis Peninsula. We were ambushed by these...these things. They fought like demons. My lord Michael was injured as you see. By the grace of the gods, we were able to fight our way clear and make it here," he sniffed. Malcolm glared at him.

"Did you kill all those things, or did you lead them here?"

"I swear, they are dead. Please, can she save Lord Michael?"

"Right now, Kari is your only chance," Malcolm growled. Jonah came running in with several sheets.

"Good, Jonah. Start tearing them into strips. I will need bandages and rags to clean him up." Kari smiled encouragingly at the pale boy.

"Don't let the prince die, Kari. Father said he was our only hope," Jonah whispered in a small voice.

"I will do my best, Jonah. Run and fetch my sewing pouch, or if you can't find that, a long straight knife. You two, be useful and stoke up the fire," she ordered. They moved numbly to the fireplace and began to do as she asked. "Malcolm, get the rest of his clothes off, see if he's injured anywhere else. Then, put the horses in the back. We can't leave now."

"Yes, Kari," he said simply as he began cutting away Michael's breeches with her abandoned knife.

Chapter Nine

Michael stared up at the unfamiliar ceiling and tried to recall what had happened. He remembered riding with Gregory, Max, and Killian toward the Ichthis Peninsula. Something had happened. What was it? He wracked his foggy brain for the answer. Suddenly, it came to him: the attack of corpses, the frightened horses screaming and plunging. The swords flashing and his friends yelling as Gregory's head parted from his torso and rolled into the underbrush. Then, the horrible stabbing pain in his shoulder. Michael reached up with his right hand and touched the bandage. What had happened after?

"You are awake?" a relieved voice said from the doorway. A young maiden stood there, looking at him. "I feared you might catch fever. We have no healer, but I did the best I could."

"Who are you? Where am I?" he asked through dry lips. She walked over and poured him a tankard of water from the pitcher by the bedside and handed it to him. After he had drunk his fill, she poured more and set it within easy reach.

"I am Kari, proprietress of the Emerald Swan. You are in Havildadt, in my inn," she paused. "Are you really Prince Michael?"

"Yes, milady, I am. And I thank you for all your help," he smiled up at her and she felt her heart flutter. His large blue eyes glowed amiably beneath bushy blonde eyebrows. His long, straight nose quivered slightly as his sensuous red lips parted slightly over pale teeth, and a dimple deepened in his right cheek. He brushed his long blond hair from his face unconsciously, and Kari was struck by how much he looked like Jackie. She blushed.

"Anyone would have done the same," she demurred, tidying up the sheets.

"I doubt that, in these times. My companions, are they well?"

"Aye, well and worried. The younger, Killian, he has been rounding up supporters, people who aren't afraid to fight. I'm afraid you don't have many, just yet. Here, let me look at your wound," she said, unbinding his bandage. Kari tenderly touched the sewn skin, feeling for warmth, and he watched her face as she probed. With his eyes, he traced the graceful curve of her throat, the smooth line of her nose, the swell of her tan cheek, and the curl of her long dark lashes. A sharp pain shot through his shoulder and Michael winced, sucking in a sharp breath. She jerked back out of arms reach, her face pale and it was almost as if she expected a blow of some sort. "I am sorry. I didn't mean to press so hard. It seems to be healing well."

"It wasn't that painful, Kari, just unexpected," he tried to smile reassuringly underneath the lie. He wanted her to come back, to touch him, again. The thought shocked him.

"I will go get something to clean and rebind it. I won't be long. Are you hungry?" Kari asked, backing toward the open door. He nodded. "Then, I will bring you something to eat, too." She turned and not quite ran. Minutes later, Max walked into the room, carrying a chair. He looked Michael over anxiously.

"She said you were awake. I am glad to see it," he set the chair by the bed and sat on it. "You have been unconscious for three days under her care. I thought we might have to travel to another town and find a real healer."

"I am doing well, my friend," Michael assured him. "Tell me what has gone on."

"Killian's sweet personality almost got us thrown out into the street, but Kari decided to help us anyway. We have been scouting the surrounding areas, rallying the people where we can. Havildadt is the anus of the kingdom, a small port town about three hundred leagues from the Ichthis Peninsula. There used to be a good-sized population here, but most of the people took to the seas when word came of the Chimera taking the throne. We got lucky, the proprietress and her family were just about to pack up and leave when we got here."

"Why did they stay?"

"She wouldn't leave until she was sure you were going to make it. Her brothers aren't the least bit happy about it, but they are cordial people who take good care of their guests. They want to talk to you as soon as you are well enough," Max stopped as a grimace passed over Michael's face.

"Just a twinge," he sighed. "Are they close by?"

"They are both downstairs."

"Fetch them for me, will you?"

"Yes, milord." Max hurried out of the room, pausing on the stairs to let Kari slip past with a tray. She smiled at him, and he nodded politely as he would to any court lady. She walked carefully to Michael's room and eased sideways through the door to carefully set the tray down on the chair that Max had vacated.

"First, I want you to drink this," Kari said firmly, handing him a chipped cup full of amber liquid with small bits of leaves floating atop it. Michael took it and sniffed cautiously, and she laughed. The sound caught him off guard, a rich and floating laugh that made him smile at his own temerity. "I assure you, Prince, that I did not work so hard to save you to poison you now. It's only spiced brandy to help with the pain. I need to clean your wound before I rebind it."

"I meant no disrespect," he said, sipping the warm brandy. She cocked her head and looked at him.

"You court people sure are a queer lot that you have to worry about it being disrespectful to worry about your life. Now, me? I would have just asked if you were trying to kill me and not worried about what you thought," she shrugged.

"There's something to be said for the world beyond court," he agreed. He drained the cup and handed it back to her and she set it back on the tray. "I wanted to learn more about the common people."

"Is that why you weren't in the castle?" she asked, pouring a pungent clear liquid onto a cloth.

"Yes. I was visiting Violet, another port town about two hundred leagues to the east of here when word came," he stopped. Kari's eyes were warm and sympathetic as she began to wipe the cloth gently along the sutures in his shoulder.

"I didn't mean to cause you grief. I'm sorry for the loss of your father. I think that all in all, he was a good king. This part is very red, so this will probably sting badly," she warned before she began rubbing the bottom of the incision. Michael gritted his teeth, but didn't make a sound. She finished as quickly as she dared, then bound a fresh linen pad over the stitches. "Still hungry or did that make you queasy?" His stomach growled in answer and she smiled, holding out a bowl of meat with thick gravy and a hunk of bread. Kari pulled the chair closer to the bed so he could reach the fruit and cheese that still lay on the tray. "Eat slowly, but eat as much as you like. I will be back later to check on you."

"Thank you, Kari," he sighed around a chunk of meat. She gathered the dirty bandages and left, passing Jackie and Malcolm in the hallway. She raised an inquiring eyebrow as she slid past but kept walking. They entered the room and stood at the foot of the bed, waiting for Michael to acknowledge them. "Gentlemen, please sit down and tell me what is on your minds."

"Well, it's like this, you see," Jackie stammered and Malcolm nudged him in the ribs with his elbow.

"We know that you are trying to gather an army and we want to join, to help. We've discussed it, and we think that the Emerald Swan would be a great place to use as a military base. You see, it has tunnels underneath it that lead to the sea below, and there are some that we haven't even explored, yet. No one knows about them, we didn't even tell Kari," Malcolm blurted out. Michael nodded.

"But, there's something you want in return."

"We are going to take Kari and Jonah, a boy who we are taking care of, to the Peninsula first. We've been talking about it, and no one in Havildadt knows what you look like as a prince. And, well, you look enough like me to be family," Jackie pushed the hair off his forehead and realization dawned across Michael's face. He smiled broadly.

"So, your cousin, perhaps, takes over the inn while you go on a trip. Our people can arrive and leave by tunnel, not creating too much suspicion, and if we can employ some boats we could have an emergency escape route by sea," Michael mused. Jackie and Malcolm both sighed in relief.

"I told you he would get it," Jackie said, proudly.

"I will give you a missive to take with you, it will give Kari and Jonah, you said? It will give them safe passage aboard any vessel to the islands and she can present it to the king there for protection. She will be an ambassador for us. And you can gather volunteers for our army there," Michael nodded, excitedly. "I never believed in the gods, gentlemen, until now. Surely, we were meant to join forces against the Chimera and put him back in the ground. Can you fetch me parchment and ink? I would write the missive while the words are fresh in my mind."

"Of course. I'll go buy some right now," Malcolm agreed. Jackie stayed a moment longer.

"Is there anything I can get for you?" he asked, hesitantly.

"No. Your sister is very lucky to have two brothers that care so deeply for her." Michael tore a hunk of bread and dipped it into the gravy.

"She's not my sister, she's Malcolm's. We just...grew up together," Jackie shrugged. "If you need anything, knock on the wall, we'll hear you downstairs."

"I will. Tell me, what's your name?"

"Oh, I'm Jackie."

"Just Jackie? No surname?"

"Orphans don't have surnames, your highness. Only dreams of something better. If you must have one, you could call us all Swans. Get some rest, sire," Jackie turned and walked out. Michael settled back and finished his bowl. Malcolm returned a short time later with the writing supplies, looking troubled.

"What is it? What have you heard?" Michael demanded.

"The Chimera has resurrected the Hunt. Those that served him before. The one's that ride on flying werebeasts? They've been spotted in the sky at night, and they are tearing the countryside apart. Rumor has it, they are looking for someone," Malcolm shuddered. "People are locking themselves inside their homes all over the kingdom. Women are disappearing. The last one was just fifty leagues to the northeast of us."

"They are looking for me," Michael said, grimly. "Give me the paper, Malcolm, and then go ready yourselves for the journey. You must get Kari and Jonah to the safety of the islands."

"Even that may not be far enough if the rumors are true," Malcolm muttered under his breath.

Chapter Ten

The wind blew fiercely through the glade, setting the hanging corpses in the trees dancing in an eerie tableau. The smell of fear and death hung thickly in the air, almost palpable enough to slice with a dagger. Dorgath scratched his mounts ears and it purred like thunder beneath his hand. Its massive tail twitched back and forth, sending small puffs of dust into the air when it landed. Dorgath shook his head. He was failing in his mission and the Chimera did not tolerate failure. He turned over his plan again in his mind. Splitting into teams of two had seemed the best idea, the more ground that could be covered, and bringing them back to this base for his inspection had seemed downright inspired. Unfortunately, the women in the northern regions shared the same auburn hair and the women of the south dyed theirs with henna and root dyes to achieve the same glorious color. He watched as one of the werebeasts batted a huge paw playfully at a girl's corpse as it swayed in the wind. There were a hundred at least, hanging amid the dark leaves. What if he had missed her? What if she were one of the danglers? The Chimera had said alive and unspoilt. He would not be kind if the girl was among the hanging. The werebeast roared, suddenly, leaping up to wrap its powerful limbs around the girl's body. The tree limb cracked beneath its weight and they tumbled to the ground.

The beast snuffled, shaking its great head, and then it began to feed. It tore with teeth and claws until it was thoroughly covered in blood and gore. It slurped hungrily, pausing repeatedly to lick its' chops. In minutes, there was only a small pile of broken bones left and it stretched out on its stomach to gnaw them contentedly. Dorgath pushed the beast off his lap and rose to prowl among the hanging corpses. When he had assured himself that she was not among them, he stalked back to his mount and sat down beside it again. There was a screeching cry from overhead and a werebeast glided into the center of the glade, bearing its rider effortlessly to the ground. The Hunter dismounted and the beast prowled into the shadow, joining it's' mate where it lay crunching a leg bone. The Hunter stalked to where Dorgath sat and saluted.

"Good news, Captain. There is another who fits your description close by. One of the captives in our last raid remembered a girl like that moving into his hometown of Havildadt a season ago. She and two brothers bought the inn there," he reported.

"Brothers? What of the brothers?" Dorgath demanded intently, his eyes starting to gleam.

"One fair, the other dark. Malcolm, he said. And Jackie," the Hunter ticked the names on his fingers. "And, oh yes, and Kari," Dorgath shot to his feet, startling the werebeasts who set up a tremendous howling roar.

"Havildadt! We must reach it by nightfall!" he grinned. "Kari is the one we seek. We must send word to the Chimera; we are on her trail!"

Chapter Eleven

Jonah leaned against Jackie's back, snoring softly. The day was drearily hot and sticky, the true dog days of summer. He almost longed for the cool of fall, but after spending so much of his life in the cold he couldn't bring himself to. Kari rode behind Malcolm, her eyes closed, a dreamy smile on her lips. She was finally warm. They had never been able to keep her warm enough as a child. She opened her eyes and smiled at him.

"I love the southlands, Jackie," she sighed, dreamily. "You and Malcolm were right with all your stories. I feel like I will never be cold, again."

"Didn't we promise you that?" Malcolm chided playfully.

"You also promised to give me the moon for a ball and the stars for jacks," she reminded him. Jackie grinned.

"You said you'd settle for an inn, as I recall, and we got you a seasick swan."

"Now, don't you go tearing down my home, especially while I am away," she warned. "I'll be coming home and that place had better be in just as good of shape as I left it in."

"You really understand, Kari, right?" Jackie asked and she nodded.

"You can't be worried about me, Jackie. Besides, someone needs to take care of Jonah. The poor kid's been through enough. Maybe he and I will collect seashells on the beach and make necklaces out of them for you. Our heroes." She looked up at the darkening sky and frowned.

"We've made good time today, covered a lot of ground," Malcolm mentioned casually.

"Maybe we should find a place to stop while it's still light enough to see?" Kari asked. Jackie strained forward in the saddle, trying to move without dislodging his passenger.

"Malcolm, what is that?" he asked, pointing to a cloud of dust along their path.

"Looks like a horde of men marching this way."

"Soldiers?" Kari asked, wide eyed, but Malcolm shook his head.

"Too ragtag to be soldiers. No rhythm to the march. Let's turn off the road and wait for them here," Malcolm turned his horse off the trail and they dismounted. Jonah was awake and watching the approaching cloud apprehensively, now. Kari touched his shoulder.

"It will be just fine, Jonah. You'll see," she promised him before taking one of the packs off the packhorse. She shared out the cheese and bread inside it and they munched quietly, watching the cloud draw closer. The sun sank to the horizon and Kari built a small fire for Jonah. They could hear the sound of footsteps now as the group grew closer. Suddenly, they hailed by from the road.

"Hello, over there! Put out that fire before you draw the demons of Hell upon yourselves!" a grizzled man shouted to them. The group halted behind him and Malcolm estimated there were about fifty of them, all battered and tired, covered in layers of road dust and sweat. Their leader was an older man, perhaps old enough to be Jackie's father, and there was concern under his gruff words.

"Gentlemen, please, join us and rest. What news have you from the west?" Kari called back. "We have food to share."

"Are you children daft? What in Heaven are you thinking, bringing a woman and child into this hell spawned night?!" the man cried, moving off the road and stomping out the fire. He glared at Malcolm and Jackie. "Do you not know about the Hunt? Do you not care that they carry off young women that fit this one's description? Get her out of the night and someplace safe!"

"If it's so dangerous, why are you out?" Jackie snapped defensively.

"We are trying to find Prince Michael, boy, so we can join him. Our homes and families were destroyed and we're out for vengeance. Why are you out here?" he demanded. "And with a child, too!"

"We're trying to get to the Peninsula, to get them to safety. Then, we're going back to the Prince," Malcolm snapped.

"Listen, boy, and listen good. You take the girl and boy and you ride like there ain't no tomorrow. You get them someplace where you can lock the door against the night and everything that prowls it," he ordered. "Now, tell me where we can find the prince."

"A moment, sir," Kari interrupted, gently. "Boys, over here," Malcolm, Jackie and Jonah followed her a few feet and leaned close. "They won't find the Swan in the dark. Especially if Michael went into the tunnels like we told him to."

"What are you suggesting? That we turn around and go back?" Jackie asked.

"In a way. We split up. Jonah and I will go on to the Peninsula; you two lead them back to the Swan."

"No! Hell no! We are not turning you two loose in the wilderness alone," Jackie snarled, shaking his head.

"Don't be silly, we will be fine."

"No," Malcolm snapped. "Look, little sister, I agree that you should go on, and I agree that someone needs to show them the way to the Swan. Night will be better for them to arrive because no one will be out to notice their arrival. That's why Jackie is going to take them back and we are riding on."

"Malcolm!"

"Don't argue with me, Kari. You and Jonah start sharing out some of that food to the men. We'll spread the load between the horses," Malcolm turned to the man who still stood glaring at the small group. "You, sir! What is your name?"

"I am called Red."

"Red, my brother Jackie is going to lead you and your men to where the prince is. I am going to take our sister and brother on to the nearest town. Help us separate our packs, please, and we'll be on our way," Malcolm offered. Red scratched his scar pocked chin, glanced at the sky, then nodded. He motioned his men off the road and began helping Kari and Jonah unload the horse.

"When we're done, you ride straight along the road as hard you can for four leagues. There is an abandoned farmhouse off the road to the right. You can barely see it from the road, but it is there. You get inside, girl, and you don't peep out until the night is over. And if you hear howling, girl, you get underneath something big and bulky and you pray until you don't hear it no more. You understand me?" he growled.

"Yes, sir," she promised. They had the packs divided and shared out quickly, and Kari hugged Jackie tightly, a tear sliding down her cheek. "You be careful, Jackie. Don't be a hero, you hear?"

"The same goes for you, Kari. You come back to me," Jackie whispered into her neck. He kissed her cheek and then hugged Jonah. "Take care of them, kid, they need looking after."

"Try not to get yourself hurt, lamebrain," Malcolm hugged Jackie then shoved him away.

"Just take care of Kari and Jonah, bonehead. And don't dawdle on the way back, you lazy bum, there's going to be plenty of work for you to do," Jackie said. "Get going." Malcolm mounted his horse and turned it to the road where Kari and Jonah were already waiting. They waved to Jackie and then spurred their horses off down the road. Jackie turned to Red. "Do you need to rest or can you go on?"

"Lead on, boy," Red growled around a mouthful of cheese.

Alone on the dark spire, a cowled figure watched the moon rise, fat and round. A cool breeze blew through the deserted streets, leaving errant pieces of trash chasing along in its wake. The figure clucked its tongue, raising its arm high, launching the small red falcon into the velvet darkness. It rose majestically, slicing through the sky like a tiny arrow, and soon was seen no longer. The figure watched a torn cloud skirt across the swollen face of the moon, then turned and shuffled back inside the spire. Now, it was just a matter of waiting...

Chapter Twelve

"Are you okay, Kari?" Jonah asked pushing his horse closer to hers. She wiped her eyes and nodded.

"We've just never been apart before. I'll be fine, Jonah, thank you. Malcolm! Slow down! We can barely see you!" she called. Malcolm turned around and rode back to them.

"Give me your reins. We'll attach them to each other so we don't get separated," he sighed. They quickly tied them off and set off again. "How far did he say it was, again?"

"Four leagues."

"How far have we gone?" Jonah asked tiredly.

"We should be there, soon. Just a little farther," Malcolm called over his shoulder. "Keep an eye out." Kari glanced up at the full moon, sitting swollen and baleful just above the horizon. A chill breeze lifted her hair from her shoulders and she shuddered.

"There!" Jonah shouted suddenly, pointing at the dim outline of a roof. "We almost missed it."

"Good eyes, little man. Let's get off the road and get some rest," Malcolm's voice dripped with relief as he turned his horse toward the house.

Suddenly, the wind began to pick up and an eerie howling began above their heads. Malcolm's horse screamed and reared, plunging sideways, pulling the others off balance. Jonah slipped from the saddle, landing with a heavy thud on the ground. Kari leapt from her horse and scooped him up as Malcolm looked up and swore.

"Kari, get on your horse and ride. Now!" he yelled as the shadows circled the moon and started toward them. The horses broke away from each other and galloped away, screaming in terror. Malcolm's horse bucked him off and then fled as he landed flat on the ground. Kari pulled him to his feet.

"Run!" she cried. "Run to the house. We have to get inside!" There was a sharp scream from overhead and the steady beat of wings increased as they ran through the overgrown grass toward the house. Kari pulled Jonah along, her heart pounding in her ears, and suddenly there was a loud roaring behind them. There was a loud thump as something hit the ground behind them. She could see the front of the house now, and the large shapes dropping from the sky behind it. Malcolm stumbled and Kari grabbed his arm to steady him. "Oh, Gods! Malcolm, run!!" Jonah glanced over his shoulder and screamed as a werebeast took a swipe at his leg. The beast's eyes gleamed hungrily, but not as hungrily as the eyes of its rider. The undead creature reached out his hand to grab him. Kari jerked Jonah up the steps and shoved him before her into the house, following close on his heels. Malcolm slammed the door shut and leaned his back against it, looking around the dim room. Moonlight streamed through broken windows, illuminating the broken furniture and debris.

"Kari, the table, push the table over here!" he yelled and she scrambled to move the heavy piece of furniture. The window shattered and a Hunter stepped over the sill and the door buckled inward. "Forget it, Kari, run! You and Jonah run! I'll try to hold them off!" Kari grabbed Jonah's hand and pulled him through the house as shutters began breaking all around them. Malcolm drew his sword and leapt away from the door to attack the Hunter that was charging after Kari. It met his mighty swing with a curved sword, the sound of metal on metal ringing through the cold house, and spun to face him. A blade materialized in its' other hand, and suddenly all Malcolm could do was defend himself against the hellish onslaught of flashing metal. A growl ripped the air behind him and a searing pain tore through his back. He whirled as the werebeast took another swipe at him, knocking the sword from his hand even as it lunged for his throat. Fangs sunk into the flesh, tearing through his jugular. The beast shook him angrily from side to side, slurping down his life's fluid greedily before dropping his broken body to the floor.

Kari ran through the house, dragging Jonah with her. A Hunter lunged through the doorway beside her, snatching at her hair, and she ducked, yanking Jonah to the side. The ring of metal behind them sent chills through her but she kept running.

"Malcolm!" Jonah cried.

"He can take care of himself, Jonah. Don't look back, just run!" Kari sobbed. Ahead of her in the dark something moved. "Hold on to me, Jonah, we're going through the window!" She took four great steps and leapt past a Hunter lurking in the shadows, crashing through the broken shutters of the window and into the night. She rolled to her feet, pulling Jonah off the ground. A large shape loomed out of the dark, and she screamed, shoving Jonah behind her. He cried out, pressing his back against her as another Hunter lurched up behind them. Kari turned, looking for an escape but found them cut off by growling werebeasts. "Jonah, get ready to run," she hissed. Kari threw herself at the Hunter, throwing her shoulder into his abdomen with all her strength. Its hands closed around her arms, yanking her up to throw her over his shoulder. Jonah roared, throwing himself at the Hunter's legs.

"You let her go!" he screamed and the Hunter kicked him aside like a pesky puppy.

"Jonah! Run! Run!" Kari screamed at him, struggling against the creature's grip.

"Mordreth, grab that brat," the Hunter holding her hissed, his voice like cold venom on a hot rock. "Bring him, he may be useful." The other Hunter lunged, grabbing Jonah by the hair, and drug him to one of the werebeasts.

"Aye, Captain Dorgath," it growled. Another Hunter poked its head from the broken window.

"Captain? What do you want done with the corpse?" it called.

"Bring it," Dorgath ordered, mounting his werebeast.

Kari began to scream.

Chapter Thirteen

Jackie stopped the men just on the outskirts of Havildadt. The town was peaceful and dark beneath the sparkling sky and the ocean roared not too far in the distance. Jackie shook his head.

"What is it, boy?" Red asked.

"It's too quiet. There's no noise but the ocean. Where are the insects, the night birds?" Jackie frowned. In sudden answer, there was a triumphant howl from above their heads and they ducked into the underbrush as a handful of large flying creatures crossed the face of the moon. A pitiful sobbing wail followed after and Jackie shot to his feet.

"KARI!" he shouted, and Red jerked him back into the scrub, holding him as he struggled to get free.

"You can't help her, boy! You can't help her, now! You'll only get yourself killed!" he hissed in Jackie's ear. "You're no good to the lass dead. Now, be still!" Jackie watched the things turn north and the great wings flap against the sky until he could no longer tell one darkness from the other. Slowly the insects started to buzz again. Jackie angrily shook Red off and began searching the ground. "What have you lost, boy?"

"The name is Jackie, and I just lost my best friend and the love of my life," Jackie snarled. "There's a blackened tree stump here, somewhere. There's a tunnel underneath it that leads to the underbelly of the Swan. That's where Michael is. Help me look for it." Someone called from the woods to their right and Jackie hurried over to see the stump. He put his foot against it and pushed with all his might, and slowly the thing began to tip over, revealing a large circular hole. Jackie snatched up a stick and lit the end, then dropped through the hole with the others close on his heels. After they were all inside, Jackie pulled hard on a long rope attached to the stumps massive roots and pulled the stump back down over the hole. Grimly, he led them through the darkened tunnels, dirt and roots brushing their heads, having to stoop at some points as the tunnel narrowed. They traveled along many switchbacks and turns until finally, up ahead, they could see a flickering light and the sound of the waves became almost deafening. Jackie turned up a set of steep and narrow stairs that were carved into the rock face leading upwards for quite a pace, passing darkened passage offshoots at several levels until they came to a trap door. Jackie pounded three times on the heavy wood and then shoved with all his might. The door rose soundlessly and Jackie led them up into the cellar of the Emerald Swan. Max stood on the steps, bow ready and pointing at the door, but he relaxed when he recognized Jackie. The greeting died on his lips as the group of men filed out behind Jackie and ranged themselves along the walls.

"Where is Michael?" Jackie demanded. Max nodded up the stairway behind him. Jackie took the steps two at a time, pausing briefly to call over his shoulder. "These are recruits we met along the road. Make sure they all get out of the tunnel before you close the door," Jackie strode purposefully through the kitchen into the common room. Michael glanced up from the maps that were spread across the table before him and rose swiftly to his feet.

"Those things have Kari. I don't know what happened to Jonah and Malcolm. We met a party of recruits on the road and split up. I brought them back and the others went on. When we got to the stump door, those things flew by overhead. I could hear her screaming, Michael. I could hear her screaming and I couldn't help her." Jackie's voice broke and tears began streaming down his cheeks. "I promised her when she was little that I would always protect her, Michael. That I wouldn't let anything ever harm her. And I couldn't help her. She was screaming, and I couldn't help her."

Michael moved to put a comforting arm around Jackie's shoulder.

"We will get her back, Jackie. Which way did they fly?"

"North," Jackie sighed, shakily. He took a couple of deep breaths and patted Michael's arm. "I'll be okay, now. Thank you."

"North? They must be taking her to the Chimera. Why?" Michael mused, scratching his chin. He sat down across from Jackie and absently studied the maps.

"The lass must have something he wants. They been stealing girls of her description all over the land." Red informed him, moving away from the kitchen doors. He bowed to Michael. "Prince Michael, we come to join your army and ride against the Chimera."

"You are greatly welcome, sir. I can use all the good strong men I can get. You look tired. Take a room and get some rest. We'll talk in the morning," Michael nodded to them, then turned his attention back to Jackie. "I wonder what happened to the others, if you only heard Kari."

"Malcolm would die before he let her be taken," Jackie said, thickly. "He's undoubtedly dead."

"Go upstairs, Jackie, and try to get some rest. We'll decide what to do in the morning. We really can't help her tonight, but I promise you this: You will see her again and we will send the Chimera back to Hell where he belongs!"

Kari turned her head to the left as the wind mercilessly slashed at her face. Jonah sat rigid, clutched, like she, to the chest of a Hunter. He seemed to be paralyzed. Kari had ceased to scream, her throat too raw, now, to provide much more than the occasional broken-hearted sob. The muscles of the beast below her rippled as the massive wings beat, then held in a smooth glide. The Hunter's arm tightened about her waist and the creature banked left. Kari shuddered. The air was turning ever more chill with each beat of the monsters wings and Kari could no longer feel her toes. North. They were going north. To him. She had the sudden urge to throw herself from the beast's back. Jonah. Who would take care of Jonah if she did? He turned his head to her, suddenly, and she could see the tears frozen to his smooth cheek.

"It's okay, Jonah. I'm here," she called to him over the wind. He nodded, then looked beyond her and his body shook with broken sobs. She knew what was there, over her right shoulder. She knew and she would not look. Could not look. If she did, she would be lost. "Close your eyes, Jonah. Don't look. Just close your eyes."

"Silence, you!" Dorgath snarled in her ear and she craned her neck to look into his glowing eyes.

"Go back to Hell, worm food!" she snapped. To her surprise, he chuckled.

"The Chimera will have much enjoyment out of your spirit. We'll see how long it takes for you to break," he leered. She turned her head away, catching sight of the treetops far below them. They looked like tiny sprigs of broccoli to her. Kari clenched her jaw against the fear that welled up inside her, her fingers digging reflexively into the pelt of the werebeast. It twitched its tail in agitation. "He must like you, little one, else he'd have flipped you off. Hold to my armor, if you like."

"I'd rather die."

"Normally, I would say that could be arranged, but you are for a higher purpose," Dorgath told her. "Ah, look, our little ride is at an end. The sun rises and the spires of the Chimera's lair come into view."

Kari looked over the beast's great head to the castle rising into view. The outer walls of the town were lined with small fires, casting eerie shadows onto the dark streets. The spires rose from the castle proper in the town's center, clawing at the lightening sky with cruel fingers. Kari felt her heart rise into her throat at the sight of a lone figure standing atop the tallest spire, watching them approach. It slid inside as the beasts began to spiral downward, landing softly at the base of the spire. Dorgath lifted Kari from the beasts back and tried to set her on her feet, but her legs would not support her, and she slid to the ground. She heard Jonah curse as the Hunter pushed him through the open doorway into the spire and Dorgath growled something as he pulled her to her feet and walked her after Jonah. They climbed several sets of stairs before turning down a thankfully level passage. Kari could hear Jonah ahead of her, but he was blocked from sight by the Hunter's back. She was relieved just know the boy was okay enough to swear. They reached a set of large doors carved with symbols of the lion headed dragon, and they pushed straight through them into the throne room.

Kari stopped dead in her tracks, her feet were rooted to the floor, and Dorgath stumbled over her. Her eyes were riveted to the roaring throne and the man who sat upon it. At his side stood a man clothed in a long gray cowl, the hood back. His face was raw, exposed to the elements and, like his hands, stripped of all flesh. Kari felt the bile rise in her throat as she fought the urge to throw up. Jonah was being hauled to the Chimera's feet, kicking and struggling against his guard. The Chimera watched with amused eyes as the boy was forced to his knees. The Hunter released his arms and Jonah sprang to his feet.

"I will not kneel to a Hell spawned creature such as you," he spat. "Murderer! Demon! You have killed for the last time!" Jonah yanked a dagger from inside his boot and lunged at the Chimera. The Chimera rose to his feet and batted the boy aside like a gnat, sending him sprawling across the floor, the dagger flying from his hand. The Chimera strode after him, drawing the sword from the scabbard buckled around his waist. Kari threw herself across the room, falling to cover Jonah's body with her own. The Chimera stopped, staring down at her.

"You would throw yourself before a blade for this creature?" he asked softly. Kari swallowed hard, and looked up to meet his black eyes with a steadiness that the rest of her body did not share.

"I will not let you harm him anymore. You have already slain his mother and father," she growled.

"And my brother!" Jonah cried, wriggling beneath her.

"And our brother," she amended, holding him firmly beneath her. "I will not allow you to take his life as well. Not as long as there is life left in my body to stop you." The Chimera sheathed his blade. His eyes bore into hers and she felt the ground sliding out from under her knees. The Chimera reached down and gently pushed the hair out of her eyes and she shuddered at his cold touch.

"Your bravery is refreshing, Kari," he said and she gasped. "Oh, yes, I remember your name. I have a special debt to repay you. Shall I start, now?"

"Do as you like, I'll accept nothing from you, except your surrender to Prince Michael," she vowed. The Chimera threw his head back and laughed.

"You are cute, I will give you that," he said, turning his head as a werebeast padded into the room. Malcolm's body lay across it, arms and legs dangling lifelessly at its' sides. Kari sobbed and Jonah rolled out from under her. She clutched the boy to her, turning his face away as two Hunters lifted Malcolm's body from the beast and laid it on its' back at the Chimera's feet. "So, you will accept nothing from me? Even the life of your beloved brother? Is death any reward for one who served me so well? I think not."

"Served him? What's he talking about?" Jonah demanded, pulling back to search Kari's eyes. A tear slid down her cheek.

"We accidentally woke him up, Jonah. Malcolm, Jackie and me. I am so sorry, Jonah. We didn't know. Didn't realize," she whispered, miserably. Jonah stared at her for a long moment, his face a tortured mask of emotions, and then he wrapped his arms around her neck.

"You didn't mean to. It'll be okay. We'll make it right, somehow," he whispered into her ear, pressing his cheek against hers.

"What a touching display. All it's missing is the good older brother to make it all right," the Chimera nodded, stretching his hand out over Malcolm's body. Malcolm began to twitch, his body spasming like a fish out of water, the folds of his open throat flapping like a wounded birds wings.

"Stop it!" Kari shrieked. "Leave him alone! He's dead, leave him in peace!" She pushed Jonah aside and threw herself at the Chimera, clenched fists swinging in rage. He caught her wrist and jerked her forward, his arm sliding around her waist, holding her hard against his side. She clawed at his face and he laughed, a deep rumbling laugh that sent icy dread scampering up her spine on tiny claws. His hand moved from over Malcolm to catch her wrists and hold them over his heart. Jonah snatched up the dagger and threw himself at the Chimera, blade raised high, ready to stab. Cold fingers closed around Jonah's wrist, pulling him around. Malcolm held his wrist gently, but firmly. He swallowed several times, and his neck spasmed, making the torn skin flutter like moths wings.

"No, Jonah," Malcolm said, his voice faint with a slight whistle.

"Let him die, you bastard! Let him die!" Kari yelled, fighting against the Chimera's grip. He looked into her eyes and smiled, evilly.

"No one dies here, unless it is at my command. And I have use for a brave soul like our dear Malcolm," he hissed. "Kneel before your king, Malcolm. And your queen." Malcolm dropped to one knee; his head bowed, and pulled Jonah with him.

"No! No!" Kari denied shrilly, trying to pull away. The Chimera lowered his head and caught her lips in a crushing, consuming kiss. His tongue slid across hers, probing into the back of her throat and she gagged. He pulled back from her, his face flush with excitement.

"No one has ever tasted those lips before. I can tell mine is the first kiss you've ever received. Good. That is how a queen should come to her king. Malcolm, Dorgath, escort her to the bather and then have her robed. You should rest, my dear Kari, before you come to me, again. You will need your strength," he warned her before shoving her to Dorgath. Malcolm rose, pulling Jonah with him.

"My lord?" Malcolm hazarded. "What shall I do with the boy?"

"Make him a cupbearer for my lady. I wouldn't wish to traumatize her by separating them. But, keep him away from the knives lest he lose some appendages. Be gone," the Chimera waved dismissively. Malcolm turned and followed Dorgath from the throne room, towing Jonah behind. He tried to smile reassuringly at the boy, but the mix of terror and pity on Jonah's young face was too much for him to bear. He pushed his tightened muscles to loosen as he followed Dorgath. They reached a hallway filled with steam and Dorgath halted before a small door;1q n ws] he knocked three times. It was opened b

"This is the Chimera's queen. Ready her for his highness," he growled. "I will be back for her later." The old woman nodded, pushing the door closed. She scrutinized Kari hard in the mists.

"There, there, little one. Old Matilda isn't going to harm you," she promised in a quavering voice. "Tis ill luck you've fallen into, to be that monsters chosen. But, perhaps you will be lucky and he will lose interest in you soon enough. Let's get you undressed." Her gnarled fingers made quick work of Kari's clothes, too quick for Kari to stop. How could one so old be so quick? Kari stood shivering in the steam, hugging herself. "Oh, come now, angel. We'll get you warm and clean in no time. Just step right over here."

Matilda took Kari by the elbow and led her through the mist to a pair of steps that led down into a steaming pool. She eased Kari into the warm water and disappeared into the fog, returning seconds later with a brush and a cake of soft soap. She scrubbed Kari from head to toe, and Kari let her, too numb to object to her tender ministrations. When she was done scrubbing, Matilda rubbed scented oil into Kari's skin and brushed her hair, then wrapped her in a long silk sheet. There were three knocks on the door, and Matilda threw back her head and cackled wildly. "Perfect timing old Matilda has! Perfect timing!" She threw open the door and glowered at Dorgath. "Took you long enough. Did you die all over again?"

"Woman, I will slice out your tongue and use it as a whetstone for my blade," he growled. "Is she ready?"

"Ready as she can be, poor thing," Matilda nodded, guiding Kari through the smoke by her elbow. "You be kind to her, you hear. She's just a lost little lamb in a den of wolves, she is."

"Go back to your washing, woman and leave the queen to me," he snapped, taking hold of Kari's arm. The door clanged closed behind them and Dorgath turned on his heel, stalking down the corridor with Kari in tow. She clutched at the sheet, lifting it from in front of her feet so she didn't stumble as he hurried her along.

"Stop! Slow down!" she cried, pulling against his arm. He glared at her.

"We've not much farther to go, girl, keep up!" he snapped, pushing aside a tapestry and revealing a flight of steep stairs. He stalked up them, practically dragging her along in his wake. They passed through an open doorway into a sitting room, then on through to the bedchamber. Beside the bed was another door, and he took her through this one to another flight of stairs. This flight was mercifully short; only ten steps curving along what she surmised must be the outside wall. Malcolm stood on the small landing guarding a simple wooden door with a large iron lock. He bowed his head to Dorgath, pushing the door open. Jonah sprang from the fainting couch as Kari was pushed through the door into the room. The door slammed behind her and a key turned in the lock. Kari looked around the small room. It was semicircular, the door behind her being in the only flat wall in the room. There was a small fainting couch, a small bed, dressing table and armoire. A small table by the bed held a basin and pitcher, and a tray of food lay on the small chair that completed the dressing table.

"That's his room downstairs," Jonah said, quietly. "The only way out is through his bedchambers. Malcolm and I looked. The one window behind the bed is too small for me to get out of, and the outside of the tower is smooth as glass. The drop is at least a couple of hundred feet. Malcolm said to tell you this: He swore fealty to you in your crib, and he serves you first and foremost. He is still your brother." Kari's legs buckled, and Jonah rushed to support her. He led her to the bed and helped her stretch out amid the silken pillows. Jonah stroked her forehead. "Get some rest, Kari. It's been a long journey."

Kari pulled him onto the bed with her and held him close, and with her arms around him tightly, she fell asleep.

Chapter Fourteen

Jackie sat at the table, rubbing his forehead. It had been two long days and even longer nights since the screams in the dark and they still rang in his ears. A tankard was set down before him and he looked up at Michael.

"I've decided. To attack the Chimera now would be folly, Jackie. We aren't strong enough," Michael said grimly, tensed for Jackie's explosion.

"I know," Jackie said softly. He traced the rim of the tankard with his forefinger. "Red says they were taking girls of Kari's description. I think it's time you knew why. You see, we needed money. There was this man who offered Malcolm a lot of it if we'd only do this one small thing."

"Which was?" Michael prodded, gently when the silence stretched too long.

"Break in to a tomb. Bring back a piece of silver," Jackie shrugged. Michael sat down hard across from him. He closed his fingers over Jackie's listlessly traveling hand.

"Are you telling me that the three of you are the ones that woke the Chimera?" Michael hissed. Jackie raised his blood shot eyes to Michael's. He seemed a century older in that moment, desolation covering him like a tightly fitting cloak.

"Yes. And we were there when he woke up. He saw us. We panicked and ran. Later, we convinced ourselves that it was a drug-induced vision. One last trick by the people who put him there," Jackie pressed bloodless lips tightly together. "He was looking for Kari, because she was the one who actually pulled it out."

Michael sat in grim silence, staring at the agony as it played across the young man's haggard face. His own emotions warred within him, driving him between wanting to comfort Jackie and wanting to gut him like a fish and stake him to the Swan's roof for the carrion to feed off of. Jackie stared at him, expectantly. Michael sighed.

"Then, he has a purpose in mind for her. And Malcolm, you say, is surely dead."

"He never would have let her be taken," Jackie agreed.

"You have done a great evil, Jackie. But you've already begun paying it back. We won't tell anyone else. It will stay between us. The others won't understand," Michael said firmly.

"I've been thinking about it, Michael. You need someone inside the capital city. Someone to tell you what's going on."

"I have sent word to someone inside the castle. If she is still free, we will have all the information we will need. I need you to help me build my army, Jackie. You will go north, but you will stay to the smaller cities and towns. You will help recruit those who are willing and able to set up resistance cells against the Chimera," Michael spoke slowly to penetrate the veil of misery that Jackie had wrapped himself in. After a minute, Jackie began to nod and the color came back into his face.

"I know a lot of people up north," he nodded. "They don't like the law on normal circumstances. They're bound to hate the Chimera's reigns. And they'll stay loyal till the battle's over. Of course, then you'll have a bunch of pick pockets and degenerates on your hands, but who better to know the secret ins and outs of the cities? I'll go get packed and head out this afternoon."

"Don't you want to wait and see what news comes from the castle?" Michael asked, surprised at the sudden animation of the other man. Jackie shook his head.

"Rumor travels faster than any bird. I'll pick up news on the road," he shot to his feet and ran from the room. Michael rubbed his eyes, tiredly.

"Max!" he called over his shoulder. Max hurried from the kitchen and stopped at Michael's elbow. "Have we received a reply, yet?"

"No, Michael."

"I want you to get ready to leave. You are going north with Jackie. He needs direction and a steadying presence. And he seems to like you. Don't let him do anything foolish," Michael waved him away, and then stopped. "And take the other falcon. In case we need to contact each other."

"Yes, Michael," Max turned and disappeared through the double doors.

"Father, guide me, give me strength," Michael whispered to the still air around him. He chewed the edge of his thumbnail in agitation. What was going on in the castle? Until he knew for sure, he couldn't know the best way to act. Customers entered the common room and Michael boomed out a jovial greeting. For now, he would play the genial host, later he would be the vengeful son and usurped ruler.

The falcon floated on a curtain of air, gliding smoothly against the clear blue sky. Sunlight rippled off its brown wings and flashed brilliantly off its keen eyes. It searched the turmoil below. The streets were crowded with people and beasts of burden, furiously rolling over each other in some mass hurry. Death knights sat astride massive horses, flicking wicked looking barbed whips at the teeming masses when they threatened to become too unruly. The falcon banked sharply, soaring over the rooftops and turned toward the castle spires. It circled once, then dove straight for a vent that boiled steam into the morning air. Tucking it's wings close, it sped down the tight shaft and broke into the vapor filled room below, circling madly once before settling upon a large rack of towels. It called imperiously, once.

"Oh, mister high and mighty feather brain! So, we sees you at last. Been waiting, Old Matilda has," Matilda untied the message from around the falcon's leg and unrolled the tiny parchment. She read it quickly and shook her head. "Oh, little Michael, how tides have turned. But, don't you worry. Your old Matilda is still faithful, along with many others. We'll be ready eyes and ears for you." She shuffled away to a small door and passed through to a smaller chamber. Inside were a bed and a writing table. She pulled clean parchment from the cluttered table and began to write, carefully applying sand and blowing it away out the tiny slit in the wall that served as a window. She rolled the message tightly and returned to the falcon. It ruffled its feathers impatiently as she tied the message back to his leg. "You speed well and fast to his majesty. You tells him quick that he can count on his old Matilda, but that his girl can't be helped"

She cautiously slid the shutters open and glanced around. There was no one to be seen. She whistled sharply and the falcon leaped into the air, flapping gracefully from the room and back into the open air. In minutes, it was a mere speck against the blue sky. Matilda turned back to the steam just as the door opened and Malcolm came in. He nodded his head to her, respectfully.

"Miss Matilda, are you ready for Kari?" he asked.

"You just brings her when she is ready. I'll take good care of her," she nodded. Malcolm tipped his head to her, again, and left. Matilda shook her head sorrowfully. Such a nice boy, to be under that monster's thrall. And his poor sister. She was a sweetling, too. Oh, yes, Matilda would help her little Michael as much as she could, and she would be as kind as she could be to the girl, as well. She busied herself with adding flower petals to the waters.

Chapter Fifteen

Kari sat on the edge of the bed, staring into space. The circles beneath her eyes screamed testimony that she had not slept well in days and her complexion had grown pale. She heard Jonah pacing by the door, restless as a small tiger in a cage, but she just couldn't gather the strength to speak to him. Suddenly, he stopped.

"Footsteps," he warned, his head cocked toward the door. Her stomach tightened. It was him. He was coming for her, as he had promised. It had been days since she had seen him, but she had heard him below, prowling his room much like Jonah prowled theirs. The door rattled, then swung open. She turned her bleak eyes to the figure standing on the threshold. Malcolm. She sobbed and threw herself across the room into his open arms. He held her close and tight as she cried into his shoulder, tenderly stroking her hair. When she had cried herself out, he gently held her away to look into her eyes.

"I am so sorry, little sister. I have been searching for a way to get you out of here, but time has run out. You must come with me to the bather once more," he stopped. She looked up at him, her eyes narrowing.

"What aren't you telling me, Malcolm?" she asked softly. He looked at the floor. "Tell me!"

"You are to be prepared for your wedding. He is only waiting on you, now. Everything else has been prepared," he said, miserably. Kari looked at Jonah, who had grown paler than death.

"I won't go," she said, simply. Malcolm shuddered.

"I was ordered to bring you to the altar or bring Jonah's head. There is a death knight waiting at the foot of the steps to carry out the sword stroke." Malcolm looked into Kari's face again. "I am so sorry, Kari." Kari swallowed hard, placing a finger to his lips.

"You are not to blame. I pulled the nail from his chest, I should pay the price. Just know that the months that we owned the Swan were worth it. It was nice to be free. Besides, maybe as his queen I can find a way to protect others from his cruelty," she kissed his cold cheek. "I love you, Malcolm. You are still my favorite brother." A ghost of a smile played across his face.

"I'm your only brother," he sniffed.

"What about Jonah?" she asked. He nodded.

"Well, him, too, but I was here first." Malcolm glanced at the boy. "He's to be bathed and dressed to attend you. We should go, before Talberth gets antsy and decides to come up."

They followed Malcolm down the steps to where the other death knight waited, and passed him without a word. Outside the chamber door, a werebeast rose from its languid stretch to pad down the passageway behind them. Malcolm whispered from the side of his mouth, "That is Destroyer. She's the Chimera's pet. She is always outside his chamber door." They walked side by side in silence, Kari squeezing Malcolm's icy hand in hers. Jonah walked slightly behind her with Destroyer and Talberth close on his heels. Jonah tried to count doors and turns but he was soon thoroughly lost and gave up. They turned a corner and steam swirled into the corridor before them. Malcolm paused to knock on the door, then opened it and bowed to Kari. The back of her hand brushed his cheek, coming away wet, as she walked through the door. Matilda was waiting by the sunken pool. Kari curtsied to her and the woman smiled as the door closing firmly behind the girl.

"Be no reason for that, sweetling. Old Matilda ain't no lady. Are you ready, up here?" Matilda asked, tapping her head.

"As ready as I can be, I think," Kari shivered and Matilda nodded, sadly. She glanced at Jonah.

"Over in the far corner, boy, there is a door just by the towel rack. Inside is a smaller bath for you. Already laid your clothes on the chair in there. Begone, now, so I can get the lady ready." Jonah looked uncertainly at Kari and she nodded encouragingly. He disappeared into the swirling steam. Kari shimmied out of the robe she was wearing and stepped to the edge of the pool. Large flower petals floated atop the slightly steaming surface. "Flowers to help calm you, my sweet. To help ready you for what's to come. I have some brewing in a drink for you, too. To make it not so nightmarish. Put yourself in old Matilda's hands, child. She'll help you through this mess."

"Thank you, Matilda," Kari sighed, stepping into the warm water. She sat down and dunked herself under the water. When she surfaced, she asked Matilda softly. "What would he do if I drown myself? Or slice my wrists open?"

"Call you back from the dead, child, and never let you know peace," Matilda sighed, running her hands through the wet strands of Kari's hair. Kari closed her eyes. "That's right, sweetling, rest while Matilda takes care of you."

Chapter Sixteen

The Chimera paced beneath the black rose covered arch. All had finally been prepared to his satisfaction. He glanced over the rows of chairs with their black silk bunting draped along the aisle, each seat filled with a festively bedecked person. Black roses covered the center aisle, a plush carpet for his lady to walk on. The courtyard was covered in black and gold decorations, tulle and satin and bows, and the fountain in the center ran with black and gold streams of wine. A roar from the far end of the courtyard made him stop. Destroyer stood for a moment, until she was sure that all eyes were on her, then began to slowly pad down the aisle. The musicians seated behind the arch took up the cue and began to play. Kari stepped into the courtyard and the Chimera smiled.

The black silk of her gown clung enticingly to her body, traced and tied at the waist with gold ribbons, falling away in a midnight train behind her. The black lace veil hung from the burnished copper ringlets atop her head, cascading down like the curls across her shoulders and down her back. In her hands, she clutched a bouquet of roses made from gold. Jonah stood behind her, dressed in gold tunic with black breeches, and he stooped to pick up the train of her gown. Kari took a deep breath, and then began to walk down the aisle, her black slippered feet crushing the roses beneath them, sending a wafting perfume up in her wake. She paused every few steps, handing a rose to this person or that as the mood took her. The Chimera frowned, but said nothing. She made her way slowly, elegantly to his side, pausing to bestow her last rose on a girl of maybe seven who wept in the front row. Kari kissed her forehead and dried her tears, smiling encouragingly at her, and then turned to face the Chimera. Her breath caught.

He stood regally on a small slightly raised platform. He seemed so much taller than six foot seven inches as she looked up at him. His long black hair was brushed away from his face in waves, like raven wings, and curled along his shoulders. His tunic and breeches were the softest of black leather, golden threads tracing designs across them like lightning. The leather bulged tightly across his muscled chest, straining to contain the thick muscles of his arms. His cheek was shaved smooth between the trace of beard along his cheek and jaw, and the hair across his chin was trim and neat. The ebony chips of his eyes devoured her as she stood below him, and he raised a hand toward her. For a fleeting moment, terror crossed her face and she tensed as though she might run. Destroyer growled softly from where she stood at the Chimera's side and Jonah leaned forward.

"It's okay, Kari. I'm here," he whispered. Kari took a deep breath and lifted her hand to place it in the Chimera's. He smiled, pulling her firmly up onto the platform to his side. Kari looked up into his eyes and found herself drowning in the darkness there. She tried to pull away, but his hand held hers in a steady grip, allowing her to go nowhere, and Destroyer padded into position at the platforms foot, just behind Kari. A young man in the garb of a priest stood before them speaking, but Kari couldn't make sense of what he said. It all sounded so garbled and far away, and she just wished he would stop his endless droning. Suddenly, there was silence, and the Chimera nodded to her. She looked around. Everyone was waiting, watching her expectantly. His grip on her hand tightened, painfully. She looked in bewilderment at the priest, whose terror was almost palpable. In desperation, he mouthed words at her, and she remembered what she was supposed to do.

"I do so promise," she repeated his words, and the gathered audience seemed to sigh in relief. Then, the priest was droning again, and all she could think about was the flower petals in the drink Matilda had given her. They had been so sweet and fragrant, and Matilda was right, she certainly didn't feel afraid. She didn't feel anything. Just annoyed at the droning priest.

"I do so promise," the Chimera said, his voice booming across the courtyard.

"I present to you, the Chimera and his Queen!" the priest called, and the courtyard erupted into forced cheers and applause. The Chimera pulled her against him and visited a ravenous kiss upon her lips that lasted until she felt she would smother. He pulled away, lifting her into his arms.

"Enjoy the feast! I have a famine of my own to break," he called to the crowd, then leapt from the platform and carried Kari back inside the castle.

'You will feel no fear, no pain, only pleasure.' Matilda's voice echoed in her ears as he carried her up the stairs. Kari sighed against his shoulder, staring back the way they had come, watching disinterestedly as Destroyer followed along in their wake. The Chimera paused as the waiting guard pushed open the doors to his chambers, then he carried her swiftly inside.

"Now, my sweet, you will learn the pleasures of married life, and its duties," he promised her, laying her among the cushions on the bed. He untied the bodice of her gown, slipping the satin from her silky flesh. He began kissing her neck, following the curve of her throat down to the hollow of her breast. He spent time caressing and learning her body, waking the warm flesh beneath his fingers to new sensations. Her small gasp as he entered her nearly sent him over the edge, but he held back and took his time, enjoying the feel of her heat and the tiny shivers that ran through her. When he finally could hold back no longer, he collapsed beside her and drew her onto his chest, where she lay curled like a small child, and he kissed the top of her tousled head. "Sleep, my kitten. We'll have more of the same when you've rested a bit. You'll enjoy it much better the next time. I promise."

Kari drifted into exhausted sleep. Beneath her head, the steady thump of his heart became the thump of a drum, and she whirled along in chaotic dance with a tall blonde with laughing eyes. The sound of his laugh brought a newly learned warmth to her stomach, and she sighed contentedly as Jackie leaned down to kiss her still tingling lips…

Chapter Seventeen

Jackie sat on the edge of the fountain, watching the crowded marketplace as he chewed thoughtfully on an apple. Married. The news had swept the land like the Chimera's soldiers. Married. A fate even worse than death. Jackie bit into the apple again, tearing off a hunk. By all accounts, Kari was fine, adjusting to her new place in the food chain. Jackie wouldn't worry about her anymore. They had things to do. Jackie rose, tossing the half eaten apple to a small child who was staring at him with ravenous eyes. After a second thought, Jackie tossed him three copper marks, too, laying a finger against his lips. The child snatched the pieces out of the air and secreted them in his dirty shirt. Jackie turned to walk away.

"Wait!" the child cried. Jackie turned back. "You the one from south?"

"Maybe," Jackie frowned. The child moved closer to him, standing almost on Jackie's toes, and motioned him to lean down. Jackie bent, a hand firmly locked on the pouch at his side. He'd played the old 'secret telling' card a few times in his youth, and had come out with several unsuspecting pouches. The boy looked around, nervously, and then licked cracked lips.

"You been trying to get support against the king," the boy half whispered. Jackie's eyes narrowed and the boy swallowed hard. "You been ratted on to the Watch. They's watching you. Getting ready to nab you, maybe tonight, maybe tomorrow. Seeing who you lead to."

"How do you know this?" Jackie asked, and the boy smiled wide showing a mouthful of broken and rotted teeth.

"Cuz I'm one of your followers," he said proudly.

"If you're one of my followers, why tell me?" Jackie asked, suspiciously, and anger passed across the boy's face. He spat in the dirt beside his foot.

"Because, they're supposed to be my partners, and they pay me with the table scraps they won't feed their dogs. You, you just gave me an apple from your own mouth and money, and you don't know me from the Chimera," the boy shrugged. "You seem like me, somehow."

"I was you. Tell me, do they know anyone else?" Jackie asked carefully. The boy shook his head.

"You're good. Can't tell who you know, or how you pass your information. I think you used to be a thief. Am I right?" the boy asked. Jackie nodded. "Thought so. Always got to help a fellow thief."

"That we do," Jackie agreed, fishing a few more coins from his pocket. He pressed them into the boy's hand. "What's your name?"

"Scurb."

"Interesting name. Tell me, Scurb. Is my lodging under watch, too?"

"Oh, yeah. From the inside. Innkeepers trying not to lose his place, so he rats on anybody he thinks might be worth something." Scurb nodded, putting the new coins with the old.

"My thanks, Scurb. You go get a decent meal. And eat it slow," Jackie tousled the boy's filthy hair and walked away. Sliding through the crowd, he sifted through the stones in his pocket, fingering the smooth edges until his hand closed around one with six angled sides. He pulled it from his pocket and carried it loosely in his palm as he walked, unhurriedly along the market. He turned onto the main thoroughfare leading from the market to the center of the city, toward the Street of Temples. Every city had one. A line of progressively finer and larger temples, each dedicated to some god or goddess of whatever the rich and lost needed at the moment. Before the Chimera, the street was swept and clean, a guard posted to keep out the truly needy and unkempt so as not to offend the rich as they came to beg their patron saints for more and better. Now, the street was lined with refuse, human and trash alike. Beggars sat along the roadside and against the temple walls themselves, calling out in pitiful voices for aid. Jackie walked stoically past them, heading as far up the street as the piles of trash would let him go. At the temple of Anra, the goddess of children and patron of fools, Jackie went inside the cool dark of the deserted temple and bowed his head. After counting to a hundred, he turned and walked back outside into the glaring sun. A beggar sitting beside the open door to the temple thrust his chipped bowl toward Jackie and mewled pathetically. Jackie dropped his stone into the bowl and moved away at a leisurely pace. Once he was no longer in sight, the beggar rose from beside the door, stuffing the red angled stone into his own pocket. He had to move quickly.

Jackie strode into the inn and loudly ordered a bowl of stew and a mug of beer before settling at one of the tables near the back wall. He noticed the look of frank shock on the innkeepers face at the sight of him, and how at the first chance, he sent one of the chambermaids scurrying upstairs. Probably to replace his stuff in his room before he went upstairs. Jackie smiled at the serving girl who brought his food and he plopped a gold coin onto the table.

"Keep the beer coming, sweetheart. And what I don't drink, you can keep for your lovely little self," he promised, digging into the thick and lumpy stew. It was pasty and hard to swallow, and had very little taste, but he choked it all down. What he wouldn't give for one of Kari's savory stews with the potatoes and gravy, and the meat cooked just so... Jackie gulped beer to wash away the lump in his throat. He had best keep his mind on the problem at hand. Jackie had chosen this table for two reasons: its view of the door, and the small hole in the floor just beside the seat. He eased the tankard off the table and poured the beer into the hole, then raised the tankard to his lips and made a satisfied smacking sound with his lips. He waved the empty tankard over his head and the girl hurried to refill it. He did this many times, and each time she came to him, he smiled a little goofier, thanked her with increasingly slurred speech. Finally, he rose to his feet, lurching into the table with a loud crash. He smiled drunkenly at the half full room and made placating gestures with his hands. Jackie staggered across the room to the stairs and began to climb, dragging his head along the wall as he went, humming a broken tune. He reached his room and barred the door, then sped lightly to the window. The serving girl who had sped up the stairs at his return was hurrying from the inn in the direction of the constables. Jackie snorted in disdain. He quickly changed clothes, and rolled his things into a bundle, tying it to his back. He pulled his long brown cloak on over his shoulders and raised the hood over his head before stepping out the window to the thin ledge there. Jackie pulled the shutters closed and then inched his way along the outside of the building. Against the brown wall, he was undetectable. He moved slowly and carefully to the side of the inn, sliding into the cool dark of the alley, and over to the brick outline of the fireplace. He used the staggered bricks as footholds and was soon down on the ground, ducking into the shadows as someone passed by the mouth of the alley. Jackie hurried in the opposite direction.

He ducked through the crowded square at the end of the alley and took off his cloak, folding it as he went. Jackie turned down another alley as a squad of the Watch went marching by, and he sped to the blocked far end. He knelt in the littered trash, brushing it away from the wall and exposing a board roughly two feet high by three feet wide. He knocked softly six times in rapid succession, the sound of a frightened heart. The board popped loose into darkness and Jackie slid inside the building, where the board was replaced tightly. A match flared in the darkness and was touched to a candle. Max smiled at Jackie.

"I got your message. How much do they suspect?"

"Only about me. The rest of the network is safe. But, still."

"It's time to move," Max finished and Jackie nodded.

"They'll be looking for me, right now they think I'm passed out in my room. I need a disguise."

"What did you have in mind?" Max asked, frowning.

"Got a knife?"

Chapter Eighteen

Kari's eyes fluttered open and focused: on the open maw of a werebeast. The razor fangs gleamed in the early morning light and fetid breath scorched her face, making her gag. She choked back a scream and shoved backward into something hard. She rolled over. The Chimera gazed at her in mild amusement. His arm circled her waist and drew her against him, pulling her into his kiss.

"You wake up the same way every morning," he said softly and she shuddered.

"I hate that damn thing! Make it stay away from me," she pleaded. He traced her lips lightly with his tongue.

"Destroyer, go," he ordered. The beast leapt from the bed with a growl and padded to the door. "Better?"

"Yes," she said, easing away from him. He jerked her back against his chest, holding her tightly.

"To whom do you belong?" he demanded, huskily.

"To you," she answered immediately. He smiled.

"And to whom will you always belong?" he demanded, nuzzling her tousled hair.

"To you," she whispered.

"Even death will not separate us, my Kari," he vowed. "Say it."

"Even death will not separate us," she repeated, her voice catching in her throat. His hands began to roam her and she closed her eyes tightly against his shoulder.

"What a sweet year," he whispered in her ear. "I return, I conquer my core kingdom, and I take my queen. Can you believe, my love, that it has been a season, already?"

"It seems like forever," she whispered and he kissed the top of her head.

"Forever is what we will have, my love," he promised, his hand sliding beneath the short bit of silk she was wearing and, despite her fear, her body began to respond to his touch. Suddenly, there was a pounding on the door. The Chimera swore and rose from the bed, throwing the coverlets aside in fury. He stormed across the room and flung the door wide as Kari scurried to cover herself. Hume leapt back from the door, a look of panic on his oozing face. "What in the nine hells do you want?"

"Word just came, my lord. One of the rebel captains," Hume stuttered, his eyes darting to Kari and back to the Chimera. "He is within our grasp. I thought you would like to know."

"Which one?" Chimera demanded and Hume swallowed hard.

"Perhaps, we should talk about this in private," he hazarded, nodding meaningfully at Kari.

"There is nothing you may not say in front of my queen. And, make no mistake about it: she is *mine*. Now, tell me before I lose my patience," Chimera snapped.

"Jackie. He is within our grasp, even as we speak the Watch is moving in on him," Hume stuttered hurriedly. Kari blanched but the Chimera smiled.

"Send for Dorgath. I want him there to bring Jackie back. Now, go!" the Chimera slammed the door in Hume's face then turned back to Kari. "Now, my lovely, where were we?"

Jackie slid into the line of peddlers leaving the city, an empty basket slung to his shoulder. The rough weave of the basket teased his ear underneath the jagged cut of his hair. He trudged, head down with the crowd, slowly making his way toward the city gate. The Watch had missed him at the inn and now were searching the city. Up ahead, a gather of soldiers scrutinized the peasants as they passed through the gate. Jackie kept his head down and tried to act tired. This would work. He was almost out of the city.

"There he is!" a familiar voiced shouted. Hands seized him, knocking the basket to the ground, and Jackie was hauled to the side of the gate.

"Are you sure?" the captain of the guard demanded.

"Lay off me! I've done nothing!" Jackie called, angrily. The innkeeper stepped into his line of sight and pointed at Jackie's hair.

"He's changed his hair, but I'd know him. Those eyes don't lie. There ain't the like anywhere in this region!" the innkeeper smiled smugly. Jackie stopped struggling and met his gaze.

"Very good eye. Too bad you used it for the wrong side," he said, simply. A roar sounded from overhead, and the gawking crowd made a mad screaming rush for the gate as a werebeast dropped from the sky. Jackie's arms were secured behind him as the death knight dismounted and strode over to the gathered guards. He looked them over contemptuously and then turned his attention to Jackie.

"You are quite the prize. The Chimera will very pleased to have you," Dorgath chuckled. He took Jackie by the arm and led him to the beast, securing him in place with leather thongs. Dorgath turned to the captain of the guard. "The Chimera is much pleased with your effort, and you will be rewarded accordingly. Keep up the good work." Dorgath mounted his beast and it leapt into the air. Jackie swallowed hard as the ground fell away beneath him and his head swam with vertigo. He closed his eyes and began to pray.

Chapter Nineteen

Kari sat on the small throne beside the Chimera's, her legs curled under her upon the violet cushion. Behind her rose carved dragon wings of pearls and gold. She watched as the parade of people came forth for the Chimera's judgment: thieves, petty criminals, and those thought to be rebel sympathizers. She listened with only a half an ear, her mind on Jackie, when she heard her name from the foot of the dais. She looked up to see an old man, dressed in fine clothes staring at her in astonishment. His smooth face and hands brought back horrible memories and his grinding voice made her shudder.

"My little Kari!" Grams laughed between his guards. "I always knew your sweet little jewel would sleep you into a rich man's good graces."

"Who is this scum that dares speak so to my queen?" the Chimera snarled. Kari turned to him.

"This is Grams. He's the one who took us in when we were orphaned and turned us into thieves. He's why we did what we did. He was going to turn me into a prostitute," she said softly. The Chimera glared at Grams, who leered back.

"That's right; she was my Kari, first. And she won't let you harm me, because she owes me," he grinned at Kari. "Isn't that right, girl?"

"Go to hell," she said. Turning to the guard beside him, she demanded, "What did he do?"

"He is accused of trying to steal a girl from the marketplace, my lady. A toddler," he bowed his head respectfully to her. She glared at Grams and then turned to the Chimera.

"No doubt to turn her out. My lord, I beg of you, end his terrible deeds," she pleaded. The Chimera laid a hand on her cheek.

"Did he hurt you?" he growled softly and she nodded.

"He beat me, and starved me, and the only reason he didn't do more was he thought my innocence would raise the price the first time he sold me," she whispered. The Chimera's eyes flashed and he turned to a now pale Grams, who began to stammer. The Chimera raised an eyebrow and the smooth skin along Grams face split open, erupting the muscles and tissue beneath. His clothes ripped as the rest of his body followed suit, and bones and sinews cracked louder than Grams screams as his body slowly turned itself inside out. His heart pounded on the outside of his ribcage, and screams of horror and revulsion erupted from the crowd. Kari simply watched, a small smile on her face as Hume's wild eyes met hers.

"Destroyer," she said, and the beast raised its head from the foot of the Chimera's throne. "Aren't you hungry?" Destroyer looked to the Chimera, who nodded indulgently. Destroyer pounced on Grams, her teeth closing around the exposed heart, and ripped. Grams' screams ended abruptly and the body sagged to the floor. Destroyer made quick work of it, leaving only a small stain on the floor before returning to her seat at the Chimera's feet to lick daintily at her paws. Chimera reached out and caressed the back of Kari's head with an approving smile. Suddenly, there was a commotion at the back of the throne room, and the remaining people parted like a wave. Dorgath marched Jackie toward the thrones, his beast pacing behind. They stopped at the foot of the dais and Jackie looked up into Kari's eyes.

"My lord, the traitor captain, Jackie," Dorgath announced. Kari laughed.

"This is not Jackie," she scoffed. The Chimera turned to her.

"You are sure of that, my darling?" he asked, suspiciously. Kari nodded.

"My Jackie is blonde and long haired. This person is black and short haired," she waved to his head.

"Your Jackie?" the Chimera growled, his jaw clenching.

"I mean only that we grew up together," she hurriedly explained, her hand closing on his arm. "I belong to you, now, you know that. And you were my first, remember?"

"Go on," he growled, staring hard at Jackie. Jackie watched in fascination as Kari traced circles along the Chimera's arm.

"This man was identified by a reliable source," Dorgath snapped.

"And am I not a reliable source? And I could identify you as Jackie, could I not?" Kari sneered. "Unlike you, *I* know Jackie, we grew up together, and this is not Jackie. But, if you need proof, Jackie has a scar on his chest. It runs from right to left where Grams sliced him with a whip." She turned to the Chimera, catching his eyes with her sincere stare. "He was trying to stop Grams from defiling me."

"Open your shirt, peasant, if you wish to live," the Chimera growled. Jackie bowed his head.

"I would, your greatness, but my hands are bound," he murmured. Kari leapt from the throne and stalked to Jackie's side. She drew open his shirt and stood back with smug satisfaction. Jackie's smooth chest glimmered with sweat, no trace of a scar to be found. The Chimera nodded.

"Perhaps he is not your Jackie, my dear, but I want him held for questioning. Take him to the dungeon, Dorgath. I will deal with him, later," he snapped. Dorgath pulled Jackie from the room and Kari returned to her throne. She tucked her legs under her, again, and lowered her head.

"Why is my Kari not pleased?" the Chimera asked, indulgently.

"Why keep him? Is my word not good enough for you?" she asked, looking up at him from under lowered lashes. He reached out and raised her face to his.

"Your word is gold to me, my love. He is not your Jackie, but he is a rebel. He might have important information. And I can not pass up that chance. I must stop Michael and his pitiful rebellion before they grow into more than just a nuisance," he said. "Do not question my orders, again, Kari."

"No, my lord. Forgive me," she murmured, hastily. He turned his attention back to the petitioners. Kari stared sullenly at the floor for a long time until he called her name once more. She looked up into his piercing black eyes.

"You look tired, my darling. Why don't you go rest?" he offered. A smile tugged at the corners of his mouth. "You may need your strength soon."

"Yes, my lord," she murmured, rising to her feet. The hall knelt to her as she swept from the room and Destroyer rose to her feet. The Chimera clucked his tongue and Destroyer sank back to the floor as the Chimera watched the door were Kari had disappeared.

"Is your word gold, my love, or silver?" he murmured, thoughtfully.

Chapter 20

Kari walked as fast as she dared down the hallway, trying not to be too noticed. Most of the servants scurried by, their eyes dropped, and those that didn't scurry dropped careful bows and curtsies as she passed. How long would she have? Why hadn't she paid more attention to how long he took reaching his judgments? Because, they were all cruel and swift, and she couldn't bear another pleading look or desperate cry aimed at her. Sometimes, he would indulge her and grant mercy or lenience. More times than not, though, he would ignore her pleas and the punishments would be more gruesome. How many people were left in today's court? She sped her pace, turning with relief down the steam filled corridor. She pushed into the room and began to cough.

"Matilda? Are you here?" she called.

"Over here, my lamb," Matilda called from the far side of the room. Kari hurried to her.

"I need your help. They've caught Jackie and I need to help him escape. Those drinks you make, can you make one for sleeping?" Kari demanded.

"Aye, I can gives you something to put in his wine that will make him sleep. And if he should wakes up too soon, it will keep him groggy," Matilda cackled, gathering herbs from sealed jars. She talked to herself softly as she poured the herbs onto a small piece of parchment and carefully folded it. She slipped it into Kari's hand. "Swirl these in his wine, and make sure he drinks at least half. Better if he drinks it all, but half should do." Kari threw her arms around Matilda and hugged her tight.

"Thank you! Thank you so much!"

"I'll ready a disguise for your young man, too. Leave it to me. Just you be careful, girl. Just you be very careful," Matilda warned.

"I will," Kari promised. She left Matilda muttering to herself and hurried to her chambers. Jonah was pacing the room and he leapt at her when she entered.

"They've caught Jackie! He's in the dungeon! I saw them march him past!" he cried. Kari shushed him sharply, looking around to see if anyone might be spying.

"Which cell is he in?" she hissed.

"One of the small ones just off the torture chamber," Jonah lowered his voice.

"Find Malcolm, tell him I am going to drug the Chimera tonight. He needs to be ready to get Jackie past the guards. Matilda is going to provide a disguise. Now, go," she ordered. As he reached the door, she called to him. "And be careful no one hears you!" He nodded and closed the door behind him. Kari went to the bedside table and emptied the contents of the parchment into the Chimera's golden goblet. Now, it was just a matter of waiting. She changed into a simple of gown of black silk and laid her onyx cloak with the fur lined hood behind the chair next to the door.

"Destroyer!" she whispered, suddenly. She moved to scoop some of the herbs out of the goblet and dump them into the werebeasts bowl where it sat on the table. She enjoyed a nightly bowl of wine with her master; hopefully the herbs would work on a werebeast, too. Kari laid down on the bed to wait.

The sound of boots woke her to darkness and she leapt from the bed just as the door opened. The Chimera strode in, looking around as the torches ignited in their holders, and the hearth blazed to life.

"Where's the boy?" he demanded.

"I sent him on errands, my lord. Do you need him?" she asked, pouring wine into the goblet. She hurriedly poured into the bowl as well and set it on the floor. Destroyer glided past the Chimera and lapped hungrily at the wine.

"No. I just don't want any interruptions," he closed the door and latched it, firmly. Kari smiled and met him halfway across the room with his goblet.

"Your wine, my lord," she offered the cup to him and he smiled.

"You are learning your duties well, my love," he commended, raising the goblet to his lips. He paused for a heartbeat, his eyes narrowing slightly, and then drained the contents. Kari stood on her tiptoes and kissed him. "You are learning very well,"

"They are a pleasure to learn," she whispered, taking his hand and leading him to the bed where she pulled him down into the soft covers. "Although, I've never heard of a man who insisted on so much…duty from his wife before."

"I've been idle for over seven hundred years, Kari. I have a lot of catching up to do," he murmured against her neck, kissing her soft flesh. "Besides, have you ever heard of a wife who so excited her husband before?" She chuckled as his hands began to unlace her gown, wondering in a blind panic how long the herbs would take. If he collapsed on top of her, she would never get out from under him. Her plans would fail! He raised himself up and shook his great head as if to clear it. "Strange. I am suddenly so tired."

"You have had a long day, my love. Here. Lie beside me and rest for a while. We have forever, remember?" she cajoled, patting the bed beside her enticingly. He shook his head again and lay down. Kari stroked his hair, soothingly, and hummed a soft tune. Soon, his breathing deepened, and she slid off the bed. Destroyer snored softly from beside the hearth, and Kari tiptoed past her to retrieve her cloak. She pulled it tight around her, slid back the bolt on the door, and eased out into the hallway. The torches were burning dim, and she clung to the shadows, moving as fast as she dared, darting into corners and shadows when other footsteps approached.

She turned down a long narrow hallway filled with suits of armor and paused. She had not seen this passage before. Biting her lip in indecision, she was about to turn around when she heard a soft whistle from the far end of the hall. A shadow beckoned her. Kari lifted her gown and ran down the aisle to where Malcolm waited for her. He hugged her briefly and then motioned her to follow silently. He led her down through dark and twisting ways, deep into the bowels of the castle until she thought she would never find the end. Finally, they rounded a turn and there was light ahead: and the sounds of singing. Malcolm pulled her flat against the wall and slipped to the opening of the archway. He peeked around the edge.

Two guards were sitting with their backs to the door, watching as Jonah danced, shirtless and sweating, on the table before them. He tumbled backward, came to his feet, and rolled forward. He leapt up and started singing in a high warbling voice that sent the guards into another burst of laughter. They raised tankards in salute of the young jester and downed them in one swallow. Jonah balanced a pitcher on his head and dipped to refill the empty tankards. Malcolm slipped silently up behind the two men, grabbed each by the neck and cracked their heads together. The sickening sound of wet crunching echoed through the cold dungeon, and Malcolm's face took on a green tinge as he lifted the first man into his arms.

"Didn't mean to do that that hard," he muttered. "Jonah, open that cell over there. We have to get these men out of sight. Kari, Jackie is in the third cell on the left. The keys are on the table." Malcolm carried the man into the dank dark of the cell that Jonah opened. Kari snatched the keys up and ran to the cell, her hands trembling. She shoved the door open and ran inside.

"Jackie! Jackie, you have to go, now!" she called. He stepped out of the darkness and she threw herself into his arms, hugging him tightly.

"Come with me," he growled softly.

"I can't. You can escape alone. It will be harder to find just you. You have to go, Jackie. Now!" she pleaded. He pushed her away to look at her.

"What has he done to you?" he demanded.

"I'm fine. I swear. But if you don't leave now, I will lose the love of my life. I can live without hope, Jackie. But I can't live with the thought that you are dead," she insisted, pressing his hands to her face. They came away wet with tears. "We've wasted so much time, we can't waste anymore."

"Come on, you two," Malcolm hissed from the door. "We could be discovered any minute." Jackie put his arm around her and ushered her through the door. Malcolm threw a sable cloak at him. "Put that on. You'll look like one of the Watch going about your duties."

"Matilda told me where she hid his disguise outside the wall. She also put a horse and some supplies there, too," Jonah piped up, tucking in his shirt. "I'll lead him to it." Kari hugged Jackie tightly one last time and then kissed him, sweet and slow.

"I love you, Jackie," she whispered, then turned and ran. Malcolm squeezed his shoulder and then hurried after her.

"Quickly, before somebody comes. Matilda told me of a better way, a secret way. Down here," Jonah said, hurrying off deeper into the dungeon. He led Jackie to the farthest wall and dropped to his knees where he began counting stones along the wall. "Ah ha! Here!" He shoved mightily and the stone slid inward, revealing a passage just large enough for a man to crawl through. "It's like the cellar of the Swan. Comes out in the forest a couple of miles from here. Hurry," Jackie slid into the hole and gave the stone a mighty push. Just as it *snicked* shut he heard Jonah whisper. "Come back for her, Jackie. Come back for us."

"I will," Jackie promised the darkness. He began to crawl.

Chapter Twenty-One

Kari hurried to Matilda and bathed while Matilda burned her gown and cloak. No trace of the dungeon must linger on Kari or her clothes. They scrubbed mightily until Kari's skin was a fresh raw pink, massaging scented oils into the tender flesh, and then they relaxed. Kari thanked Matilda, again, as she dressed and then she went down to the kitchens for a snack. As she wended her way back up to his chambers, a piercing shriek suddenly split through the castle, reverberating through the very stones. Kari clapped her hands to her ears and ran, throwing herself against the door and inside, shoving it to with all her might. The sound stopped. She breathed a sigh of relief.

"Where have you been?" a deep voice growled behind her, dripping menace and anger. She turned with a startled squeak. The Chimera sat upon the bed, his back against the headboard, watching her. She wiped her mouth, which had gone desert dry suddenly and tried to smile.

"You fell asleep, so I went for a bath and a snack," she said lightly. His eyes bore into her.

"And nowhere else?" he demanded.

"Of course not," she denied, walking toward him. He raised a hand and she hesitated.

"Do you know what that sound is?" he asked.

"No."

"It's an alarm. It means that a prisoner has escaped," he bit off each word as he spoke and then he rose from the bed.

"Who?" she asked, trying to slow her racing heartbeat.

"Your Jackie, of course. Wasn't that why you drugged my wine?" he demanded, walking toward her. She held her ground, shaking her head in mock confusion.

"I didn't drug you. And that man was not Jackie," she began. His hand lashed out, catching her across the side of the face, spinning her across the room. She landed heavily against the door holding her cheek, the hot salty taste of blood flooding her mouth.

"You lied to me. You drugged me. And you set my enemy free," he snarled, stalking her slowly. "You betrayed me, *my love*." Kari shoved the latch free, but it ricocheted back into its bolt hole, and the door began to glow with heat. She shoved herself away from the door, looking desperately for an escape. The room upstairs. She darted behind the fainting couch to her left and ran for the tapestry covering the stairwell. It shimmered as she reached it and she bounced off the solid wall with a muffled ,cry landing on the floor. "You will not betray me, again, Kari. Nor will you lie to me. And rest assured that *when* I catch him, Jackie will suffer a thousand deaths. And you will watch each one from my lap." Kari pushed herself onto her hands and knees, her hair tumbling wildly into her eyes. She looked for a weapon, anything she could use against him as he paced toward her.

"Now, my Kari," he hissed, "now, you will pay the price of disobedience."

He lifted his hand toward her, his scowl drawing his eyebrows down in demonic likeness. Kari felt her muscles contract in a single cramp, drawing her legs and arms in to her sides. She tried to cry out, but her throat muscles were beyond her control. She dropped to the floor in a ball as he stopped above her, watching her with hard unforgiving eyes. He twitched a finger, and her skin began to blister and crack, her hair thinned and fell away. Her face wrinkled and sagged, the skin sliding away from the skull. Kari's muscles erupted through her thinning skin with a severe spasm, and hardened before her astonished eyes. Then, they slowly began to flake away into a fine powder. She watched as the bone of her arm grew porous and soft, and finally crumbled. Her breastbone split open, revealing her organs, and still she could not scream through the intense pain of living decomposition. Finally, her eyes withered in upon themselves, and she could see no more. She could only feel the electric, raw pain of what were once her nerves and muscles, and the rapid pounding of her heart where it lay upon her twisted and jagged spine. The Chimera reached down and lifted her heart into his hand, raising it to eye level.

"*I* hold your heart now, Kari," he hissed, his fingers closing in a slow crushing grip around her pounding heart. The organ burst between his fingers, running down his forearm to drip gore from his elbow. He opened his palm and licked it, once, languidly.

"Even death will not separate us," he vowed.

CONTINUED IN BELLEREPHON

www.ingramcontent.com/pod-product-compliance
Lightning Source LLC
Chambersburg PA
CBHW030146200626
46812CB00015B/1722